"What happened to setting the record straight?"

"I couldn't go through with it." He rubbed the back of his neck. "Not this afternoon."

"So we pretend to be madly in love? How is that going to work?"

"For now, we'll go along with the matchmakers' plan. And plan a more strategic withdrawal."

Her heart did a somersault. They were barely a breath's width apart. Her pulse pounded.

Colton touched the tip of his finger to her chin. Her world went topsy-turvy. "Mollie..." Was he having as hard a time breathing as she was?

But his hand fell away and he moved back a step. "I'll pretend we're a love match as long as necessary. I owe you more than I could ever repay for all you've done for Olly."

A sick feeling knotted her gut. Gratitude was the last thing she wanted. "You don't owe me, Colton."

So much for any illusions she'd foolishly harbored that he might view her as anything more than his best friend.

Lisa Carter and her family make their home in North Carolina. In addition to her Love Inspired novels, she writes romantic suspense. When she isn't writing, Lisa enjoys traveling to romantic locales, teaching writing workshops and researching her next exotic adventure. She has strong opinions on barbecue and ACC basketball. She loves to hear from readers. Connect with Lisa at lisacarterauthor.com.

Books by Lisa Carter

Love Inspired

Coast Guard Courtship
Coast Guard Sweetheart
Falling for the Single Dad
The Deputy's Perfect Match
The Bachelor's Unexpected Family
The Christmas Baby
Hometown Reunion
His Secret Daughter
The Twin Bargain
Stranded for the Holidays
The Christmas Bargain
A Chance for the Newcomer
A Safe Place for Christmas
Reclaiming the Rancher's Heart
A Country Christmas
Falling for Her Best Friend

K-9 Companions

Finding Her Way Back

Visit the Author Profile page at LoveInspired.com for more titles.

Falling for Her Best Friend

LISA CARTER

ISBN-13: 978-1-335-59885-1

Falling for Her Best Friend

Love Inspired
22 Adelaide St. West, 41st Floor
Toronto, Ontario M5H 4E3, Canada
www.LoveInspired.com

Printed in Lithuania

Wherefore let them that suffer according to the will of God commit the keeping of their souls to him in well doing, as unto a faithful Creator.

—*1 Peter* 4:19

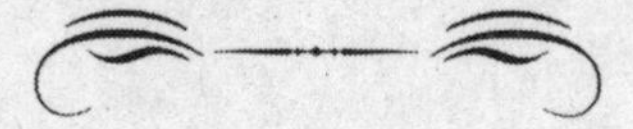

To all those who have experienced the joy
of falling in love with and being loved in return
by your best friend.

Chapter One

On that chilly afternoon in early April when her best friend stepped off the bus, Mollie Drake's heart did its usual uptick in response to his rugged handsomeness.

Drake, though, was no longer her legal name. Yet after all these months, it still didn't feel right to think of herself as Mollie Atkinson.

His eyes lifted to meet hers. For a split second, something unfamiliar swept across his chiseled features. An intensity. His blue eyes lit with a warmth just for her.

Colton Atkinson wasn't only her best friend. He was also her husband. But a husband in name only.

He reached for the little boy in her arms. Oliver shrank from Colton, his arms in a stranglehold around her neck.

Twenty-one-month-old Olly dug his knees into her side in a mad scramble to get as far away from his father as possible. "Go 'way, man."

She felt the blow to Colton's heart as if it had struck her own. This was not the long-awaited, picture-perfect reunion she'd envisioned for father and son.

In the parking lot, she handed Colton the keys to his truck, strapped Oliver into the car seat and climbed into the vehicle. On the horizon, the mountains undulated in blue-green waves.

Colton steered the red pickup across the winding road toward Truelove. "Olly doesn't know me."

She recognized the deep disappointment in his voice. They'd understood Oliver wouldn't remember his father. He wasn't even a year old when Colton was deployed. But she'd worked hard for Olly not to lose the sense of his father's identity.

When communication lines allowed, there'd been FaceTime chats with Colton. She'd told Olly about his dad's favorite foods and colors. She'd shared stories about her and Colton growing up together.

"I talked about you all the time," she rasped.

She glanced at the child in the back seat. Oliver was Colton's son, not hers. Although in every way except biological, she felt like his mother.

Olly's blue eyes—so like Colton's—scanned her face. "Da-da solder?"

Such a good, dear little boy. Her heart quailed at the prospect of losing him forever. Yet it was only right for Oliver—who'd become dearer to her than her own life—to be with his father.

"Yes, sweetie pie." She swallowed. "Daddy is a soldier."

"Not anymore," Colton grunted.

Her eyes flicked to him. She'd grown used to

seeing him in uniform. But having recently separated from the military, today he wore civilian clothing—a beige canvas jacket, a hunter-green checked shirt, jeans and boots.

Colton's gaze settled upon her like an electric bolt. "Molls, are you okay?"

She blushed at having been caught staring. "I'm fine." But she wasn't.

Ever since they were children, there'd been an inexplicable connection between them. An invisible cord binding them to each other.

As the truck ate up the miles to the small mountain town of Truelove, North Carolina, her anxiety mounted. She'd missed him so much while he'd been deployed, but his homecoming threatened to tear her world apart.

Ten months ago when he received his emergency deployment orders, she'd let her heart get in the way of her head. They hadn't thought through their impetuous decision to marry. They'd only reacted.

But his return meant nothing would ever be the same again. His post-enlistment plans to create a new life with Olly left her with a sense of sinking dread.

Colton shifted his gaze to the rearview mirror. "Daddy is so glad to see you, son."

Scrunching his face, Oliver pointed his finger at his father. "Go 'way," he yelled.

Colton flinched.

Straining against the car seat harness, Olly held out his arms for her. "Mowee! Mowee!" he howled.

"Please don't cry, honey." Unable to reach him from the front passenger seat, she wished could comfort him. "I don't know what's gotten into him."

His shoulders stiff, Colton kept his eyes fixed on the curving road.

"Oliver does know you. I have pictures of you in every room. He's just out of his routine."

Tired and hungry were a deadly combination for a toddler.

She unbuckled her seat belt. Stretching over the seat, she plucked the snack container with the circle-shaped dry cereal out of the backpack. "Hang in there, sweetie pie."

His little body hiccuped with sobs. His chubby fingers made short work of fishing out the Os. But the snack was a delaying tactic at best.

Twisting around again, she sat down and rebuckled her seat belt. Gradually, the snuffling noises subsided. Clutching the snack container, Olly closed his eyes.

"Let's pray he sleeps until we make it to Truelove." She took her phone out of the pocket of her gray jacket. "Aunt EJ wanted to know our ETA. She probably wants to bring a casserole over for dinner tonight."

Colton tossed her a crooked grin, causing butterflies to swirl in her belly. "Do you think Miss ErmaJean made her chicken casserole?"

Whether she were married, divorced or a spinster, "Miss" was an honorary title of respect bestowed on any Southern lady who was your elder. No matter how old the "Miss" was.

"Could be." Mollie smirked. "Since it's your favorite, and Aunt EJ is never so happy as when she's feeding people."

Forehead creasing, he returned his gaze to rounding a tight bend in the road. "While I'm in Truelove, maybe I should keep a low profile."

He wasn't wrong.

"Thanks for letting me spend tonight at your house. Oliver and I will get a fresh start on the road tomorrow morning."

Her heart skipped a beat. "So soon?" She'd hoped… "Stay home for the weekend."

"Truelove isn't my home." He made a face. "Much as I appreciate everything you've done for us, it won't be Olly's, either. I've got a job prospect near the beach."

Her heart pinched. She cast her gaze over to the perpetual smoky mist on the ridge of mountains from which the Blue Ridge derived its name. "But what will you do with him when you're at work? If you were closer, I could—"

"I'm not living in Truelove." A stubborn look crossed his features. The same one she often saw in his son. "I'll figure it out."

During Colton's extended deployment, she'd made a life for herself and the little boy in Truelove. But Colton had never felt the same about their hometown as she did. Maybe because he'd never had a family to call his own. He'd spent his childhood in and out of foster homes.

She twisted the plain gold band on her finger. Oliver whimpered in his sleep. Leaning over the seat, she put a soothing hand on him.

Yet it was Mollie who needed comfort. How would she ever survive without him?

Colton took a long look at the woman beside him. Same sweet, lovely Mollie. The best friend he'd ever had. The best person he'd ever known.

He shouldn't have been so abrupt with her. But Truelove brought back hurtful memories.

Avoiding his gaze, she stared out the window at the passing scenery. On one side of the road lay the majestic Appalachian Mountains. On the other, separated only by a slim guardrail, lay a cavernous gorge.

Yet somehow, when everything else in the world changed, the mountains never did. Within the month, the evergreen-studded mountain slopes would explode into breathtaking splashes of pink rhododendron, flame-orange azaleas and white mountain laurel. Despite his claims to the contrary, the land tugged at a not-so-small part of him. The closest he'd ever felt to finding himself home.

An uncomfortable silence stretched taut between them. They'd never had any difficulty talking until now. Laughing together. Sharing hopes and dreams. More often than not, able to finish each other's sentences.

When they were thirteen, they'd made a pact to never fall in love with each other and risk their all-important friendship. Then he'd ruined everything by asking her to marry him.

He preferred not to examine too closely from where the impulsive marriage proposal had sprung.

At the time, she'd been talking about moving back to Truelove to help her mom, Glenda, who'd recently been diagnosed with cancer. Only eleven months after the death of his late wife, Erin, when he received his orders to ship out to a war zone, all he could think about was making sure he didn't leave Oliver an orphan in the foster care system.

Yet he'd been shocked when Mollie accepted his marriage proposal without hesitation. Their marriage on the eve of his deployment had been for Olly's sake. A marriage of convenience.

Desperate to cut the tension, he cleared his throat. "How's your mom?"

She laced her hands together. "The final round of chemo was rough. Running the hair salon in her absence has been hectic, but between Dad and I, we've made it work for everyone."

He propped one arm on the steering wheel. "You always make it work, Molls."

"I didn't make it work by myself." She sniffed. "Truelove embraced Oliver and me into its folds. It's one of the best things about life in a small town. They take care of their own."

Problem was, he'd never been one of their own.

Always an outsider. Never fitting in. Never belonging.

Mollie's blue-gray eyes turned stormy. "While you were away, Olly never suffered for lack of anything. Everyone loves him. I love him." Her mouth quivered.

His heart wrenched. This situation was unfair to her. But once he'd learned his team was about to rotate home, a panic of a different sort had built inside his chest.

Colton wasn't sure what to do with the complicated emotions he felt for his best friend, who was now his bride.

What had he been thinking when he'd asked her to marry him? He scrubbed his face with his hand. He *hadn't* been thinking. Only reacting from a deep gut-level instinct he'd spent months trying to unravel in his head.

After descending into the valley, the truck emerged onto gentler terrain. Split-rail fencing lined the roadside. Horses grazed in the pastures. Truelove was known for its orchards. The apple trees were beginning to leaf out.

He squared his shoulders. "It's obvious Oliver is a happy, healthy little boy, thanks to you." It was killing him to hurt her like this. "But we talked about this on the phone. Leaving is for the best."

"For Olly? For me?" She laughed, the sound entirely without mirth. "I don't think so."

"You'll thank me in the long run." He pinched the bridge of his nose. "The marriage was a temporary fix. None of this is real. We aren't real, Mollie. Better to rip off the bandage than to prolong the agony."

She flipped her long brown hair over her shoulder. "Good to know marriage to me is agonizing."

"That's not what—" He took a steadying breath. "It was selfish of me to ask you to take on Oliver's care with everything your family is going through. I'm trying to put things right."

She threw out her hands. "This is your idea of putting everything right?"

He stared blindly out the windshield. He was no good at relationships. His brief, rocky marriage to Erin illustrated why he needed to steer clear of romantic entanglements.

Olly startled awake. "Mowee?"

His thumb stuck in his mouth and tears silently trekked down his cheeks. Colton's heart broke. The last thing he'd ever wanted was to hurt his beloved boy.

Whimpering, Olly held out his arms to her. "Take, Mowee. Take."

"Don't cry, sweetie pie." Once she'd unbuckled her seat belt, she reached over, swiping the tears from the little boy's face. "I can't take you right now, but Mollie's here."

Not for long, though.

Was it too late for him and Oliver? Despair settled like a heavy mantle over his shoulders. "Olly hates me. Maybe he would be better off without me."

* * *

Mollie's stomach tanked.

This wasn't what she wanted. Not for Oliver. Not for any of them.

"Olly doesn't hate you. He's a frightened little boy, who needs a chance to get to know his dad again. If you take him now, you'll only frighten him more. You could permanently damage your relationship."

Colton stiffened. "He's my son." His voice went sharp. "Not yours."

She met his gaze head-on. "I think I've earned the right to tell you what I believe is best for Oliver. Let him learn to trust you—to love you—in his own time."

Colton's hands strangled the wheel. Oliver wasn't the only one frightened. Traces of ten-year-old Colton with an enormous chip on his shoulder and massive insecurities remained in the man next to her.

Yet somehow, even as a child, she'd been able to see past the surly attitude and nearly impenetrable walls to a boy worth knowing.

She took a breath. "Will you consider staying in Truelove for a while?"

His face shadowed. "What difference will it make if I stay?"

"It's not like you to give up so easily."

"How long are we talking?" A bleak pain darkened his expression. "A few days? A few months?"

"Until Olly feels comfortable and safe with you."

She jutted her jaw. "Figuring it out as we go is what you and I do best, right?"

"What happened to the girl who liked to weigh the pros and cons?" He cocked his head. "The girl who always looked before she leapt?"

She shrugged. "I met you."

For a moment, he stared at her. Then he laughed. "When have I ever been able to say no to you?"

Lots of times. But that street ran both ways. "It's going to be all right, Colton."

"I've made such a mess of things. First with Erin. Now with Oliver and you." His Adam's apple bobbed in his throat. "I have no business trying to be anyone's dad."

Unsure what he meant about his late wife, she frowned. "I'll help you get reacquainted with Olly. I believe in you, Colton."

"You always have." He shook his head. "When no one else bothered."

"There are a lot of people in Truelove who care about you."

He flicked her a look. "Why do you care so much?"

"Because I—" She clamped her lips shut against the word from which there was no return. "Because that's what best friends do."

"I'll stay." He straightened. "Only until the end of spring, though. My buddy will hold the job open for me for a few months." His eyes bored into hers. "But after that, no matter what, I'm leaving Truelove with my son."

The suffocating heaviness eased in her chest. She'd managed to avoid losing Oliver today. But Colton returning to Truelove unraveled a whole new set of unforeseen problems.

How was she going to tell him everyone in Truelove believed their marriage wasn't born of convenience, but of love?

The knot in her belly tightened. It wouldn't take long for her family to grasp the true nature of her sham marriage. Her parents' marriage was a shining example of love and devotion. They would be so disappointed in her for hiding the truth of her relationship with Colton.

She tucked a strand of hair behind her ear. "I need to tell you something before we get to Truelove so you won't be blindsided."

He stiffened. "You've met someone." There was a strange hollowness in his voice.

"Why would you think—" She turned toward him. "No. That's not it."

A muscle ticked in his jaw. "What is it then?"

"Everyone assumes we fell in love after Erin died, and that we decided to get married before you deployed."

He darted a glance at her. "Including your parents?"

Biting her lip, she nodded.

He rubbed the back of his neck. "But we called them right after the ceremony to let them know I was deploying and that we'd gotten married."

"I guess they heard what they wanted to hear in

the order they wanted to hear it." She knotted her hands in her lap. "By the time I drove the U-Haul with Olly from the base to Truelove, the whole town knew we were married. People jumped to the wrong conclusion."

"Why didn't you set them straight?"

Heat crept from underneath the collar of her jacket. Why hadn't she?

Because everyone in town had assumed she and Colton were a foregone conclusion. Because feeling the pressure of her singleness, she was too embarrassed to admit the only reason Colton had married her was for the sake of his child.

"I—I just didn't," she stammered. "Mom was sick. Dad was so stressed. They were thrilled at the news." She took a ragged breath. "I'm sorry for letting everyone believe a lie."

She'd always made it a policy to tell the truth. When it came to Colton, though, she no longer was sure what was true and what was false. Everything was so mixed up in her heart and in her head.

"You were dealing with a lot." He lay his hand, palm down, on the seat between them. The long-ago friendship pact had included a strict no-PDA policy. "We'll set the record straight first thing."

Her parents would never understand. She didn't understand what had induced her to marry him. Actually, that wasn't true. She had her suspicions.

She placed her hand, palm down, onto the truck seat beside his. Side by side. Only their pinkies touching. Something they always did. Adhering to the no-touching clause of their friendship pact. Yet also a reassurance that between them all was well.

He threw her a boyish, lopsided smile and her heartbeat quickened.

The pickup clattered over the bridge into town. With spring runoff underway, the rushing river foamed below the bridge, bending around the small town like a horseshoe. Reaching Main Street, Colton braked sharply. Jolted forward, she caught hold of the dashboard.

Parked catty-corner across the street, a Truelove Fire Department engine blocked further access to downtown. A giant American flag hung from the fire truck's extended ladder. A row of firefighters in turnout gear came to attention and saluted.

He threw her an incredulous look. "What in the world…?"

Wafting in a slight breeze, a banner hung across Main: *Colton Atkinson—Our Hometown Hero.*

She gasped. *Oh, no.* So much for keeping a low profile.

Cheers erupted. It appeared as if the entire citizenry of Truelove had turned out to welcome them. Lining the sidewalks on both sides of the street, dozens of people waved tiny American flags.

On the village green, the high school marching band broke into a rousing rendition of John Philip Sousa's "The Stars and Stripes Forever."

Colton looked as dazed as she felt.

Her insides nose-dived. *Aunt EJ, what have you done?*

* * *

Beyond the fire truck, the storefronts lining Main Street were draped in patriotic bunting like the Fourth of July.

Colton scowled. "For the love of red, white and blue, what's going on, Mollie?"

Why were they doing this for him? Mollie had been his only true friend in town. Hadn't she?

"Fire twucks!" Oliver pressed his face against the window. "Me wuv fire twucks!"

At the sharp rap on his window, he and Mollie jerked. Mayor Watkins, who doubled as the jolly old elf during Santa on the Square every Christmas, beamed at them.

"Santa!" Olly shrieked.

Mollie chuckled.

Colton glared. "This isn't funny, Molls."

Grinning, she glanced over the seat at his son. "Your daddy knows Santa, Oliver."

Colton rolled his eyes.

She smirked. "Just trying to increase your street cred with your son."

Mayor Watkins whirled his finger, and Colton pressed a button. The window rolled down.

"On behalf of the good citizens of Truelove, welcome home, Sergeant Atkinson." The mayor's snow-white beard glistened in the afternoon sun. "The fire department would like to provide you with an official Truelove escort on the final leg of your journey home."

Colton flicked a look at Mollie. No help there.

Her shoulders shook with suppressed laughter. "Sure, Santa. Whatever you say."

Watkins waved at his son. "You continue to be a good little boy, and Santa will make sure you get something special for Christmas." The mayor squeezed Colton's shoulder. "Although Olly's already gotten the best present ever—his father home from war."

A lump formed in Colton's throat.

Stepping away from the truck, Watkins motioned for the fire chief. "Let's get this celebration started!"

Lights flashing and horn blaring, the fire engine rumbled down Main Street.

"Yay!" Oliver yelled.

Hero status made Colton uncomfortable. The real heroes were the soldiers who hadn't made it home. But for his son's sake, he followed the fire engine at a slow, careful distance. As they passed, people broke into applause.

Colton looked at Mollie. An amused smile tilted the corners of her lips. Olly waved at everyone.

He recognized a few faces from high school. It appeared most of his former classmates had spouses and children of their own. They had real families and real marriages. Unlike him.

"I don't get it, Mollie." A cold, hard feeling settled like a stone in the pit of his stomach. "Why are they doing this?"

"Everyone is so proud of you." She touched

his shoulder. "I'm proud of you." A citrusy scent floated past his nostrils, tantalizing his senses.

His pulse ratcheted up a notch. In those months before he was deployed, Mollie had come on weekends to help him—a suddenly single parent—cope with a newborn. And the girl he'd known most of his life had proven to have a curiously deleterious effect on his resolve to keep their relationship friends only.

At the corner of the square, the fire truck veered right.

"Don't tell me we're going to circle the square," he moaned.

Mollie winked at him. "You're getting the full VIP Truelove welcome."

"Such as it is," he muttered.

But her smile felt like a ray of sunshine. Warming places in his heart he'd believed forever cold. It had been a long ten months since he'd last seen her. He'd missed her so much.

The procession wound its way past the town hall and the police department. Another hard right. They drove past the library. The empty bay of the fire station.

"Kids, Mowee!" Excitement laced Olly's voice.

"I see them, sweetie." She leaned forward on the edge of the seat to get a better look. "Oliver adores other kids."

Waving flags, schoolchildren ringed the playground at the elementary school. The same playground where, once upon the disaster called his childhood, Colton had met a little girl named Mollie Drake.

Her mouth curved, and he knew she was remembering, too. Something almost painfully sweet banged inside his rib cage. Funny, how so often they could read each other's thoughts.

Colton steered around the next corner. "Did you know about this?"

"I had no idea. Although last week, Aunt EJ asked me a bunch of questions about when your bus was due at the station."

He groaned. "Where there is one…"

She threw him an apologetic look. "This has the Double Name Club written all over it, doesn't it?"

The Double Name Club—notoriously known as the Truelove Matchmakers—was infamous for its members poking their powdered noses where they didn't belong.

GeorgeAnne Allen. IdaLee Moore. ErmaJean Hicks was Mollie's great-aunt.

The seventysomething ladies took the town motto—*Truelove, Where True Love Awaits*—a little too seriously. The matchmaking double-name cronies were determined to help everyone in the small Blue Ridge town find their happily-ever-after.

Whether the recipients of their efforts wanted them to or not.

One more right turn and they were on Main Street again across from the Mason Jar Café.

"Not much the matchmakers can do about us.

We beat 'em to the punch." He arched his eyebrow. "Fake or not, we're already married."

The sudden eclipse of her smile left him feeling a ridiculous sense of loss. She turned away from him. He told himself to remember the pact. First and foremost, they were best friends. Anything more wasn't possible. Not if it meant risking their friendship.

Colton had the acute, unassailable conviction that without Mollie, nothing might ever be right for him or Oliver again. Yet the fear—a fear he wouldn't, couldn't, give a name to—was so strong. He had to leave. Leave before it was too late.

Too late for what? His pulse thumped. He was beginning to suspect it might already be too late.

Chapter Two

With a final horn blast, the firefighters waved for Colton to pass into Mollie's neighborhood.

She turned toward his son. "What did you think of Daddy's parade?"

He bounced in his seat. "Fun, Mowee."

The oaks formed an arching canopy over her street. In one of the older neighborhoods in Truelove, the Craftsman bungalows had been built for a different generation of GIs returning from war.

Colton steered into the driveway of the house Mollie inherited from her dad's mother. Growing up, she'd spent a great deal of time here. Which meant he had, too.

With a personality as sunny as Mollie's, her grandmother Drake always made him feel welcome. Somehow, it felt like he'd come full circle in the best possible way.

He was thankful Oliver had spent the last ten months of his life in such a nurturing place. Now it would be up to Colton to ensure the new home he created for Olly was as loving and safe as the one his son would soon be leaving.

Once she got out of the truck with Oliver in her arms, she ambled toward the porch. He retrieved his duffel bag.

Smiling, she unlocked the front door. "I think someone else will be mighty glad you're home, too."

Truelove wasn't his home. How many times must he remind her before she—

Mollie swung open the door. Fluffy tail wagging, his dog barked.

"Bwoo!" Olly fidgeted, but she held him in a firm grip.

Colton's chest tightened. Had Blue forgotten him, too? But with a scrabble of his nails, the merle-coated border collie with bright blue eyes rushed onto the porch and launched himself at Colton.

Dropping his gear, he took a knee on the step and embraced the excited dog. Blue slobbered over his face in a flurry of welcome.

Mollie jiggled the little boy on her hip. "See how excited Blue is that Daddy's home."

He bit off a sigh. He never managed to remain peeved with her for long. "Thanks for taking good care of my kid, my truck and my dog, Molls."

She batted her lashes. "Sounds like the makings of a hit country ballad."

Laughing, he gave Blue's head an extra rub behind the ears.

Her phone dinged. She set Oliver on his feet. Reading the text, she chewed her lip. "Aunt EJ's on her way." Flustered, Mollie tucked a loose tendril of hair behind her ear, an old nervous habit. "The Double Name Club's coming along for the ride."

"We're beyond their matrimonial machinations." He raised his shoulders a notch and let them drop. "What more can they do? For once, they've been outplayed."

Her eyes went wide. "Don't let them hear you say that. It's tantamount to daring disaster to strike."

Resting a light hand on Blue's head, he rose. "Let 'em do their worst."

She shuddered. "I don't think you appreciate the calamity you're inviting upon us."

Her great-aunt's lime-green Honda CR-V pulled into the driveway behind his truck. Blue barked a welcome. Laden with insulated food carriers, the three ladies extricated themselves from the SUV.

Colton caught hold of Blue's collar. Unconsciously or not, Mollie moved closer to his side. A peculiar sensation unfurled in his chest.

"It's never a good idea to underestimate them." Her gaze flicked to him. "Something's been up with them ever since Aunt EJ found out you were coming home."

For the love of applesauce, Truelove wasn't his—

"Gigi!" Olly clapped his hands.

Mollie shot Colton an apologetic look. "My cousin Ethan's kids call her Gigi, so he does, too."

"Nothing wrong with that." He leaned against the porch railing. "It's not like Erin and I have any great-grandmas to give him."

His son toddled down the steps to greet the ladies.

"It's okay to let go of Blue." She held up her hand. "Blue. Sit." The dog sat on his haunches.

He threw her a grin. "I'm impressed."

"As you should be." Her eyes sparkled. "Olly's still a work in progress, though."

He gave her a crooked grin. "As am I."

She rolled her eyes. "Ain't that the truth."

He hurried to take the casserole travel container from Mollie's great-aunt. "Is this what I hope it is, Miss ErmaJean?"

The pleasantly plump older woman, who'd never met a stranger, laughed. "If it's chicken casserole you're hoping for, your hopes have been fulfilled. As have my prayers for your safe return. Hand that to my niece and hug my neck."

He obliged, and Mollie's great-aunt held him tight for a moment before releasing him. She smelled of cinnamon sugar. Her denim-blue eyes suspiciously moist, she patted his shoulder. "So good to see you, honey."

Oliver tugged at her pant leg. "Cookie?"

Mollie pursed her lips. "It's not polite to ask Gigi for a cookie every time you see her."

"Cookies are one of the things great-grandmas do best." ErmaJean reached into her voluminous quilted handbag and handed Oliver a napkin-wrapped sugar cookie almost as large as his face. "Here you go, sweet boy."

Mollie shook her head. "You're spoiling him, Aunt EJ."

ErmaJean fluttered her hand. "The other thing great-grandmas do best."

Olly sat on the bottom step to enjoy his treat.

"We should put the food in the kitchen." Mollie's great-aunt collected the other carry bags from her friends. "We'll be right back."

She and Mollie disappeared into the house. An enticing aroma of good eats lingered in the air behind them. Colton's stomach rumbled.

It had been a long time since breakfast at the base in Fayetteville this morning. One thing he'd give the Double Name Club—theirs was a generation who knew how to cook. He looked forward to dinner.

"Colton Atkinson, my dear boy."

He turned to the oldest and most diminutive of the Double Name trio. "Miss IdaLee."

The retired schoolteacher had taught four generations of Truelove's children, including him and Mollie.

She touched his sleeve. "Let me be among the first to wish you and your bride as much happiness as Charles and I have found together."

According to Mollie, the octogenarian and her long-lost beau had been a romance sixty years in the making.

Mollie and ErmaJean rejoined them.

IdaLee's violet-blue eyes shone. "Your impromptu wedding reminded me of my childhood. I always thought it was sooooo romantic when a dashing soldier married his sweetheart on the eve of shipping out to war."

Dropping her gaze to the gray planks of the porch, Mollie twisted her fingers together. He'd hoped to talk to the Drakes first, but with the True-love grapevine standing in front of him, perhaps it was best to get this misunderstanding taken care of now.

He cocked his head. "About that…"

Never one to remain silent for long, the final member of the compatriots-in-mischief grunted. "Speaking of romance, young man."

The angular, faintly terrifying woman with the ice-blue eyes and short, iron-gray cap of hair was as spare as Mollie's great-aunt was round. The uncontested leader of the matchmaker pack, GeorgeAnne was the bossy one—although in his opinion, that was splitting hairs.

He stiffened. "*Were* we speaking of romance?"

Once upon an adolescence, he worked as a stock boy in the Allen family hardware store. He still had no idea what had prompted the cantankerous older woman to hire a foster kid like him in the first place.

Now like two prizefighters in the boxing ring, they warily eyed each other.

After a second, the corners of GeorgeAnne's thin lips flattened in what for her passed as a smile. "We most certainly were speaking of romance, which is the reason we're here today."

"And bringing dinner," ErmaJean pointed out.

Irritation flickered across GeorgeAnne's bony features. "As I was saying..." She threw ErmaJean a look.

Mollie's great-aunt made a show of zipping her lips.

GeorgeAnne opened her hands. "For the great service you rendered your country, the Double Name Club has decided to help you and your bride celebrate the romantic milestones you missed as newlyweds."

He reared a fraction. "Romantic what?"

GeorgeAnne looked at him as if he didn't have the sense God gave small animals. "You missed the six-month anniversary of your wedding."

ErmaJean smiled, the crow's-feet fanning out from her eyes. "And your first-year anniversary is coming up in a few months."

IdaLee lifted her index finger. "We also mustn't forget you missed celebrating Valentine's with your sweetheart."

He glanced at Mollie, whose cheeks flamed fire-engine red.

"Valentine's Day was months ago." He directed a glare at GeorgeAnne, the force of nature who doubled as the town's chief mayhem maker. "It's April."

"Exactly." ErmaJean clasped her hands under her double chin. "What could be more romantic than celebrating Valentine's Day under an arbor of apple blossoms?"

"Spending quality time together is important."

The afternoon sun cast dappled shades of light onto IdaLee's snow-white bun. "Charles and I are firm believers that weekly date nights enhance affection."

GeorgeAnne made a face. "I'm sure none of us need to hear any further details about your *marital* affections, IdaLee."

He knew better than to laugh. "The thing is, Miss GeorgeAnne—"

Mollie sprang in front of him. "It was so sweet of you to plan this lovely…lovely…" Her gaze sought his.

"Surprise?"

Mollie nodded. "Surprise for us, but you see—"

"Don't you worry your pretty head, honey bunny." Her great-aunt smiled. "We've already ironed out the details. Only thing you two have to do is enjoy yourselves. Starting with joining the family Easter egg hunt tomorrow on the square."

Not much of a churchgoer—as in rarely ever—Colton had forgotten his return coincided with Easter weekend.

He and Mollie exchanged glances.

Colton broadened his chest. "We really can't—"

"The more the merrier." GeorgeAnne pointed to the GMC pickup pulling up to the curb in front of the house. "I'm sure Mollie's parents have a few things they want to say to both of you."

Beside him, Mollie wilted.

His tail whipping the air like a flag on the Fourth of July, Blue barked a greeting to Glenda and Ted Drake. Oliver jumped up from his perch. He took off at full toddler speed, running to meet them with Blue at his heels.

Scooping Olly into his arms, Mollie's dad tickled his belly. Colton experienced a pang of envy that his son wouldn't allow him to do the same. Laughing, the little boy squirmed with delight.

The change in Mollie's mother made Colton wince. Glenda's reddish-brown hair was gone, replaced by a colorful purple headscarf. A loss perhaps especially painful for a hairstylist like herself.

She'd always been slender, but there was an air of fragility about her. Over the years, Mollie's bubbly mother had treated him like family. The family he'd never had but always yearned for.

His eyes welled.

GeorgeAnne jabbed a sharp elbow into his ribs. "None of that. She's as much a warrior as you. Give her the respect she deserves."

So much had changed, but Glenda's eyes in her too-thin face were the same vivid green.

Riding high on Ted's shoulders, Oliver lunged for Mollie's mom. "Wenda!"

"Not so fast, Olly, my boy." Ted caught him just before the child face-planted onto the grass. "Only hug her legs and be gentle."

"Me careful. So Wenda not break."

The lanky general contractor set Colton's son onto his feet.

With the same care he might cradle a baby bird, Oliver wound his pudgy arms around Glenda's jeans. "Me happy to see you, Wenda."

The lump grew in Colton's throat. Blue settled comfortably between the trio of them at the base of the steps.

Colton and Mollie moved to join them.

Glenda's fingers combed through Olly's soft baby curls. "I'm happy to see you, too." Turning toward Colton, she cupped his face in her palms. "I'm also oh so glad to see your father safe and sound."

Her hands felt paper-thin and cool on his skin. But her smile… Like her daughter's, her smile had the ability to light up the world. His world, at least.

"My darlin', darlin' boy has come home to us at last."

He struggled to speak around the boulder in his throat. "It's good, so good, to see you, Miss Glenda."

"Don't you worry about me, soldier." Patting his cheek, she gave him a tender smile so like Mollie's it nearly brought him to his knees. "I'm tougher than I look."

"Ain't she just?" Ted winked. "Not much gets my boss lady down." Mollie's dad pulled him into a bear hug. "I can't tell you how pleased Glenda and I were when you called to tell us you two had gotten married, son."

His heart pounded. No one had ever called him "son." If ever he'd had a father, he couldn't imagine anyone more wonderful than Ted Drake. There was no man he respected more. Which only made the situation more uncomfortable.

IdaLee put a soft hand on Glenda's back. "Everyone always knew those two were meant for each other."

Not true. He recalled more than one concerned citizen warning Ted to steer his daughter away from a troublemaker foster kid like Colton. But seeing more in him than he could see in himself, the Drakes took him under their wing and set a place for him more nights than not at their dinner table.

His pulse hammered. Once Ted and Glenda knew the truth, the affection they'd showered upon him would change to a well-deserved fury. Her father would be justifiably irate that Colton had taken advantage of Mollie's good nature.

Colton braced for a punch to the face.

Worse still, their pretense of a marriage would devastate the already-delicate Glenda. A bead of sweat broke out on his brow.

"Like two peas in a pod," ErmaJean said.

"Joined at the hip," IdaLee agreed.

GeorgeAnne snorted. "We were beginning to think Mollie never would find a husband."

Colton went rigid. Mollie wrapped her arms around herself. For the first time, he considered how the truth would humiliate her in the eyes of everyone in town.

He and Olly were leaving, but she'd be the one to bear the brunt of his ill-considered marriage of convenience.

Colton stepped toward her. "Mollie."

Pivoting toward Ted, she took a deep breath. "Daddy..." A Southern girl called her father "daddy" from birth to death. Her death, not his. "I need to tell y'all something."

Ted slipped his arm around her. "Everything okay, Mollie girl?"

The expression on her face gutted Colton. A roaring filled his head. He couldn't do this to her. Not this way. Not right now.

He tugged her against his side. She threw him a startled look.

ErmaJean tilted her head. "What was it you wanted to tell us, honey?"

He crooked his pinkie around hers. "My bride and I just wanted to thank you for welcoming me h-home." He cleared his throat. "We'll look forward to the date nights and—"

"What are you doing?" she hissed.

She placed her hand on his chest. The warmth of her fingers traveled through the fabric of his shirt. Did she feel his heart jackhammering?

GeorgeAnne's mouth hardened. "And what?"

He locked eyes with his best friend in the whole world. Who was also his wife.

Colton lifted his chin. "Mollie and I will see you at the Easter egg hunt tomorrow."

His bride?

Mollie blinked at him. Where had that come from? His about-face on the issue of coming clean left her dazed.

But soon after, her parents departed. Her mom didn't have the strength yet to be out for long periods of time. To Mollie's immense relief, Aunt EJ and the Double Name Club left, too.

Working off pent-up energy, Oliver and Blue chased a ball around the yard.

She whirled on Colton. "What happened to setting the record straight?"

"I couldn't go through with it." He rubbed the back of his neck. "Not this afternoon."

"Then when?" She folded her arms. "What happened to ripping off the bandage?"

He pinched the bridge of his nose. "I couldn't lay that on your mom today."

"So we pretend to be madly in love? How is that going to work?" She shook her head. "A make-believe marriage isn't sustainable. How long are you proposing—" She blushed. "How long are you willing to go along with this farce about romantic milestones?"

"I don't know."

"And what if my mom never..." Her voice broke.

He seized hold of her pinkie again. "Your mom is going to get through this. And so are we. You, me and Olly."

Pulling free, she tucked her hands underneath her arms. "Everything feels so out of control." *She* felt out of control.

"For now, we'll go along with the matchmakers' plan. And plan a more strategic withdrawal. On a timetable of our choosing."

"You sound like such a soldier," she huffed.

The corner of his lips tilted. "Thank you?"

Her heart somersaulted. They were barely a breath's width apart. Her pulse pounded.

Colton touched the tip of his finger to her chin. Her world went topsy-turvy. "Mollie…" A muscle ticked furiously in the hard line of his jaw. Was he having as hard a time breathing as she was?

But his hand fell away, and he moved back a step. "I'll pretend we're a love match as long as necessary. I owe you more than I could ever repay for all you've done for Olly."

A sick feeling knotted her gut. Gratitude was the last thing she wanted. "You don't owe me, Colton."

So much for any illusions she'd foolishly harbored that he might view her as anything more than his best friend.

At a sudden gust of wind, she shivered. Clouds scudded across the sky.

She called Oliver and Blue to come inside. Colton grabbed his bag. She ushered them into the house. Olly headed to his toy chest in the living room. Blue padded after him.

After he'd been deployed, she'd replayed every conversation she'd had with him, stretching back to the weekends she'd traveled from her job in Raleigh to the base in Fayetteville to help with Olly.

Sifting. Searching. She'd puzzled over what prompted his out-of-the-blue marriage proposal. At the time, it had seemed life had come right side up for her.

Yet there could be no doubt it was fear—a fear

for Oliver after his mother's death—that prodded Colton into doing something he regretted.

What was the old saying? *Marry in haste, repent at your leisure.*

She did not question he cared for her. His willingness to spare her public humiliation was proof of that. In his own way, he loved her.

But as a friend. Mollie was beginning to hate that word. And the silly friends-only pact they'd made as teenagers.

Once Colton left town with Olly, Truelove would be abuzz with questions. One of the least positive aspects of life in a small town. There'd be so much fallout.

She'd have to deal with it alone.

This afternoon, he'd bought them a reprieve. Crisis averted for another day. Until then, no one must suspect the truth about their marriage of convenience.

Perhaps it might be prudent to take a page from Colton's life playbook. It went against everything true to her nature. But in the days ahead, however long or short her time with him, maybe she should take steps to safeguard her heart.

Standing inside the door, Colton surveyed the house she'd moved in to when she and Oliver returned to Truelove.

"What do you think of what I've done with the place?"

Her grandmother Drake's house had been a safe

haven. Colton's foster family—with whom he'd lived until his enlistment—had lived two doors down. He'd long since lost touch with the kind, if overwhelmed, foster parents. They'd moved away. He had, too.

He poked his head out the door again. "The siding's gray, not white."

She rolled her eyes. "Thank you, Captain Obvious. The house needed updates. Anything else you notice?"

Nothing ever stayed the same, but he was pleased the strain between them had evaporated. They were on familiar footing again—best buddies, pals through thick and thin. "You painted the door turquoise."

"It's called robin's-egg blue." She smiled. "Sam Gibson painted it for me."

Something unpleasant pinged inside his chest.

Mollie shut the door. "Remember Sam? He played on the football team."

Colton shifted the duffel strap on his shoulder. Gibson had been from the same wrong side of the tracks as him. Through his talents on the football field, Gibson fitted into Truelove, yet Colton never managed—nor wanted—to bridge the gap.

He also recalled the girls at school found Gibson easy on the eyes.

Colton crossed his arms. "Does Gibson go around painting everybody's door or just yours?"

She shrugged. "Not everybody's. But a lot of people's doors."

"Thought you'd be smarter than to fall for that."

She looked at him like he'd lost his mind. "Sam's been a good friend."

He jutted his jaw. "When were you planning to tell me about your *friendship* with Sam Gibson?"

"I'm friends with Sam and his wife. She used to be Lila Penry."

He blinked. "The artsy girl?"

"As a paint contractor, Sam was a such a blessing to me when it came time to refresh the exterior."

"Gibson's a paint contractor?"

Maybe he'd jumped to the wrong conclusion. He'd often wondered why none of the guys in Truelove had snapped up Mollie before now. He'd always laid it to their inability to recognize a good thing when they saw it.

In high school, he'd lived in dread of the day one of them noticed her. When he'd lose his place in her affections. Or she became too busy for him. It had never happened, but it remained a sore point.

"Sam and Lila live in the house with the apple-green door down the block. Olly likes playing with their daughter, Emma Cate." She glanced into the living room to check on the little boy. "I think she's practicing to be a big sister. Lila is expecting a baby over the summer."

Bypassing the kitchen, she led him across the hall to the guest bedroom. "Oliver's bedroom is close to mine at the back of the house. Will this room work for you?"

"It's great."

The bedroom was light and airy with a large window overlooking the side yard. He placed the duffel on top of the navy blue comforter.

"I should see about warming Aunt EJ's casserole for an early dinner. I'll leave you to get settled." At the door, she paused. "You didn't think Sam and me were dating, did you?"

Colton flushed.

"As if." Fluttering her lashes, she held up her left hand. "I'm a married woman, remember?" She laughed and left him to unpack.

It had been a confusing day, beset with unexpected complications. But her casual remark set him pondering. Time had not stood still for either of them.

He was not the same person he'd been before spending ten months in a global hot spot. She was different, too. The new forthright Mollie disconcerted but also intrigued him.

A myriad of conflicting emotions, including guilt, overcame him.

Had his rash proposal kept her from finding love? If she hadn't spent the last few months married in name only to him and caring for his son, would she have been in a relationship with someone else?

Colton sank heavily onto the mattress.

Imagining her with someone—anyone—felt like a kick in the gut.

Chapter Three

Overnight, the temperature dipped.

Colton awoke to a strange white light filtering in from outside. After getting dressed, he brushed aside the curtain to find a light covering of snow on the ground.

In the kitchen, Mollie poured him a cup of coffee. Her pink sweater brought out the reddish tints in her hair she inherited from her mom. She looked good, but she always looked good to him.

He rubbed the back of his neck. "I didn't mean to sleep so late."

She handed him the steaming mug. "Yesterday was exhausting."

He smiled at his son strapped into a booster seat at the kitchen table. "Hey, Olly."

Oliver gave him a dark look before spooning oatmeal in his mouth.

"Exhausting in more ways than one." He warmed his hands around the ceramic mug. "I didn't expect to see snow."

"Springtime in the Blue Ridge." Her mouth

curved. "Next week, the forecast calls for temps in the sixties."

He took a sip of coffee. "Is the Easter egg hunt still on?"

She inserted a slice of bread into the toaster. "A little snow won't keep Truelove from its annual egg hunt."

Midafternoon, they donned their coats. It didn't take long to walk to the square. Nothing was too far from anything else in Truelove.

Despite the cold, the sky was a beautiful Carolina blue. She held tightly on to Oliver. Colton carried Olly's egg-collecting basket on his arm.

The green was crowded with parents, grandparents and small children. He spotted ErmaJean and IdaLee behind the refreshment table. Clutching a clipboard, GeorgeAnne stalked about with a whistle hanging around her neck.

Colton held out his hand to Mollie. "It's showtime, Mrs. Atkinson."

She gave him a funny look, then took his hand.

Mollie introduced him to a lot of people. He made no attempt to keep track of their names. He was not going to be here long enough for it to matter.

He remembered her cousin, who was about six years older than them. Ethan had served in the US Marines before returning to Truelove. They joked good-naturedly about the Army-Marine rivalry.

She motioned to the little blond boy in her cousin's arms. "Olly, say hi to Parker." She turned toward Colton. "I told you about the tornado that hit Truelove three years ago during the egg hunt?"

Colton nodded.

Ethan shook his head. "Pregnant with Parker, my wife, Amber, the girls and a bunch of other families rode out the worst of the tornado in the Mason Jar. Then Amber went into labor."

Colton's eyes widened. "What an entrance into the world."

Ethan gave him a wry look. "Egg-xactly."

Colton grinned.

Amber, a pediatric nurse, joined them. "Dad humor at its finest."

Mollie looked around. "Where are the twins?"

"They've aged out of this preschool-targeted event." Ethan set Parker on his feet. "So naturally, Miss GeorgeAnne put them to work."

Parker waggled his fingers at Oliver.

Amber smiled at the two boys before turning to Colton. "Belated congrats on your wedding."

Ethan slipped his arm around his wife. "Childhood friends make the best spouses, right, babycakes?"

Amber caught her husband's eye. "Absolutely."

Stiffening, Mollie looked away. Colton squeezed her hand.

Perched on the steps of the gazebo, GeorgeAnne blew her whistle. Everyone gathered around. Bellowing into a bullhorn, the meddlesome matchmaker explained the egg hunt rules.

Every child was allowed to find only ten eggs

so the smaller kids like Oliver "hunted" on a level playing field with the older, quicker preschoolers like three-year-old Parker.

Mollie nudged Colton. "You help Olly. I'll take the pictures." She started to move, but he still had hold of her hand. "Oops."

With a sheepish smile, he let go. "Sorry." Yet he missed the warmth of her hand. And the way her hand fit into his.

The fake-husband thing wasn't turning out to be as bad as he'd feared.

Colorful plastic eggs dotted the perimeter of the square. Hidden behind trees. At the base of a shrub. Concealed behind a snow-dusted clump of daffodils.

GeorgeAnne blew the whistle again. "Happy hunting!"

The kids hit the ground running. He followed his son into the grass, but Oliver pushed at his leg. "Go 'way. Me do."

His heart constricted.

"Don't worry." Mollie bit her lip. "We'll keep trying."

He shrugged to show he didn't care. But he did care. Deeply. What could he do to show Olly how much he cared?

Oliver scurried toward a bright orange egg.

A dark-haired girl got to it first. "Look, Daddy!" She held it up to her doting father.

His son glared at the girl, but catching a glimpse of lavender, he dashed toward a dogwood tree.

Once more, though, another child with his dad beat him to the punch.

Olly ground to a halt, and his gaze traveled from Parker and Ethan to another little tyke hunting eggs with his father.

Most of the parents on the green were dads or granddads. Oliver's face fell as he made the connection.

"Oh, no," she whispered.

Colton's heart lurched. He understood the pain of feeling like the only one without a father. But Olly had a father who loved him and would always be there for him. Whether Oliver wanted him there or not.

Squaring his shoulders, Colton marched over to a pale yellow egg in the grass. "Olly," he said, beckoning. He guarded it, lest another child snatch the prize from his boy. "Look over here."

Basket dragging, Oliver plodded over.

Colton stepped aside for the big reveal. "See any eggs, Olly?"

With a whoop of joy, his son pounced upon the plastic egg. He cupped it in his palms and gazed upon his treasure with wonder.

Colton grinned at Mollie.

She snapped a picture. "That's a keeper."

After ten excruciating months, he ached to hold his son in his arms again, but he'd dared not attempt it after yesterday's meltdown in the truck.

He did, however, allow his hand to fall briefly upon Oliver's silken brown curls. "Good job, son."

Blue eyes unreadable, Olly looked at his father but he didn't flip out. Erring on the side of prudence, Colton didn't prolong the physical contact. Dealing with his son was like dealing with a skittish woodland creature.

He never knew what to expect from the little boy—fight or flight. "Want to look for another one, Oliver?"

Olly didn't reply, but when Colton moved away, the child meandered alongside him.

Not exactly an enthusiastic endorsement of his recon skills, but he'd take what he could get. And if he did say so himself, his Army-honed skills were spectacular.

It didn't take long for Oliver to "discover" the next one. Soon, the little boy's basket was filled.

At the end of the hunt, everyone raided the refreshment table for hot chocolate and cookies. Olly showed his finds to Parker. His son traded with Parker for an orange egg.

"I didn't realize Olly knew his colors." Colton straightened. "Is he a boy genius?"

Mollie threw Ethan and Amber a wry look. "Excuse him, y'all."

His eyebrows rose. "What?"

She laughed. "Olly is only starting to learn his colors."

"Nothing wrong with being a proud dad." Ethan clapped a hand on Colton's back. "You're a good one."

"I want to be." He stuck his hands into his pockets. "But it isn't like I had a father to teach me."

Ethan nodded. "Me, either."

Colton had forgotten that about her cousin. Perhaps they had more in common than he'd supposed.

Amber took Parker's hand and control of his basket. "See you at church tomorrow? It's Easter Sunday."

Mollie looked at him.

Glad of the excuse, he reached to reclaim her hand. "Of course." A united church front was sure to allay any suspicions about their marriage.

Parker's older sisters, Lucy and Stella, ran up and pulled at Ethan to come see something.

"Hang on a minute, girls. Colton, would you be up to doing lunch some time at the Jar?"

"I'd like that." He smiled. "Thanks."

Later at the house, he helped Mollie clean up after dinner. Oliver played in the living room with Blue.

She wiped off the countertop. "Not a bad first outing for father and son."

"It's a start." He settled his hip against the kitchen island. "How do you think my first outing as a fake husband went?"

She gave him a sideways look. "It's a start. Always room for improvement."

Colton chuckled. "Challenge accepted."

"Here's a challenge." She draped the cloth over the drainboard. "Help me give Olly his bath."

Colton followed her into the bathroom. “Will he accept my help?”

“He loves the water. Other than washing him, bath time basically involves making sure, in his overconfidence, he doesn’t drown himself.” She turned on the faucet. “Besides, he needs to get used to you in his life.”

After wrangling Oliver into the bathroom, she sat on the tiled floor and stripped off his shirt and pants. Eager to get into the water, the little boy made a break for it.

“Oh no, you don’t, mister.” Grabbing him around the waist, she held him captive in her lap. “While I wrestle the gator, Colton, how ’bout you take off his socks?” She blew a strand of hair out of her eyes.

His son glared daggers at him. But taking his cue from Mollie, he got a firm grip on Olly’s scissor-kicking feet and slipped off the little boy’s socks. “How did you manage bath time by yourself?” he huffed.

She laughed. “It wasn’t easy, but you do what you have to do.” Twisting the faucet to Off, she helped Olly climb into the tub. “Sit down, Oliver.” The water level reached his tummy. She pulled a small step stool to the tub, then sat down. “Bath first and then you can play.” She lathered a green dinosaur bath mitt.

Colton sank to his knees beside the tub. “Will he be okay without your hand on his back?”

She washed under Olly’s arms and around his

neck. "Last time we gave him a bath together was in the sink at your apartment at Fort Liberty."

Colton nodded. "He was so little and so slippery."

"He sits fine without support in the tub." She smiled. "You're a big boy now, aren't you, sweetie pie?"

Oliver handed her a red plastic boat.

She filled the open-sided boat like a cup and used it to rinse the soap off his torso. "That first time we bathed him, he was so tiny I was scared I would break him."

Colton grunted. "Me, too."

Reaching under the water, she scrubbed Olly's toes. "But what I recall most was the sweetness of those days."

He looked at her. "Me, too."

They smiled at each other.

Something stirred inside him. Her smile faltered. Dropping her gaze, she rinsed and wrung out the bath mitt.

When she tried washing Oliver's face, the child batted at her arm. "No, Mowee. Me do."

"All right. But if you don't do a good job, I'll wash your face again." Handing Olly the mitt, she slanted a look at Colton. "He's so much like you it's ridiculous."

Colton's mouth twitched. "You mean he inherited my handsomeness and winning personality?"

She rolled her eyes. "I mean he inherited your

bone-deep stubbornness and complete disregard for social niceties."

"You say that like it's a bad thing."

Olly held up his face for her inspection.

"Great job." She dumped a bucket of bath toys into the water. "You can play for a while."

Down the hall, the washer dinged. "I should get those towels into the dryer." She got off the stool.

He rose. "Let me get them."

"Spend the time with Oliver instead."

He gave her a dubious look.

"You'll be fine." She patted his arm. "Have fun." She disappeared down the hall.

With trepidation, he took her place on the stool. This was the first time he'd been alone with Olly.

Leaning over the edge of the tub, he retrieved a plastic yellow starfish floating in the water. "Do you like this one, son?"

Making engine noises, Oliver ignored him. The little boy plowed the red boat through the water in ever-widening ripples around his body.

Chucking the starfish, Colton snagged hold of a purple whale and squeezed. The toy squeaked. "Cool. What do you—"

Scooping water into the small boat, Olly sent a wave over the side of the tub, soaking Colton's shirtsleeves.

He reared. "Whoa."

Eyes fixed on his father, Oliver did it again. This time, the wall of water doused Colton's shoes. A second of shocked silence ticked between them.

"You want a water war, dude?" Colton gave him a pointed look. "You got it."

Using his palm, he propelled a surge of water over the little boy's tummy and up to his chin, careful to send it no higher.

Eyes widening, Olly sputtered.

Colton sucked in a breath. What had he done? What kind of father sloshed his kid just because the kid splattered him? What sort of example—

Oliver sent another spray over the side of the tub, drenching Colton's jeans. Yet there was mischief, not enmity, in his gaze.

Something warm, like melted butter, swelled in Colton's heart.

His son followed with another big splash. Colton splashed back. The child laughed.

Colton laughed, too, before sending a tub-size tsunami Olly's way. For a few minutes, it got wild. Back and forth. Tit for tat.

"What in the name of hair rollers is going on in here?"

He and Oliver froze.

Mollie propped her hands on her hips. "I leave you two alone for five minutes, and you wreck the bathroom?"

He and his son looked at each other. A shocking amount of water dampened the tile. The bath mat was soaked.

She crossed her arms. "I am not cleaning up this mess."

He helped his son climb out of the tub and

wrapped him in a brown towel with a fringed hood that resembled the mane of a lion.

Flicking her an oh-so-casual glance, Colton picked up one of the sponges. "I hate for you to miss out on the fun." Making sure he had her attention, he applied pressure to the sponge. Water droplets dribbled onto the already-wet floor.

She went rigid. "Don't even think about it, Colton Atkinson."

Giving her a wide-eyed innocent look, he juggled the sponge from one hand to the other. "Whatever do you mean, Molls?"

She wagged her finger. "You know exactly what I mean."

He cocked his head. "Don't you want to have fun with me and Oliver?"

She backed toward the door. "Don't you dare—"

Colton let the sponge fly. It landed on the wallpaper beside her head.

"Ha." She sniffed. "You missed."

"Mollie. Mollie. Mollie." He threw her a cheeky grin. "I meant to miss. Next time you won't come off so dry."

She narrowed her eyes at him. "What next time?"

He cocked a glance at his son. Olly handed him another sponge. Mollie's eyes went huge.

"No fair for you two to gang up on me." She grabbed the sponge at her feet. "I can throw a sponge, too. And I won't hesitate—"

He threw the sponge at her.

Screaming, she grabbed the door. Hopping into

the hallway, she slammed it shut behind her. The sponge landed with a satisfying smack on the back of the door.

Thank you, Molls.

She could have zinged them if she'd wanted to. She'd played on the girls' high school championship softball team.

He looked at the little boy. Oliver smiled. A small smile, but it was a start.

"We better mop up the mess we made, Olly." Once Colton had grabbed some extra towels, they got to work.

His heart lifted with hope. He and Oliver might just find their way to each other.

The next morning, Easter Sunday, Colton drove them to the white clapboard church. The church was nestled in a glade on the edge of town. The steeple brushed a picture-perfect Blue Ridge sky. He parked in the gravel parking lot.

Diaper bag slung over her shoulder, Mollie removed Oliver from his car seat and settled him onto her hip. Fearing Olly might cause a scene, Colton didn't offer to carry him for her. Keeping quiet, he followed them over the tiny footbridge spanning a small creek.

The temperature was rising and already the snow on the banks was melting. Water burbled over the moss-covered stones.

"I see Jeremiah." She jiggled Olly on her hip. "Let's go talk to our friends."

Colton's mouth tightened. "How about let's not?"

Oliver bounced in her arms. "Fwends."

"Friends are important, right, Olly?" She narrowed her gaze at Colton. "Stop being antisocial and make friends of your own."

He grunted. The only friend he'd ever needed had been her. But she was too much like her grandmother Drake and aunt ErmaJean.

Always the social butterfly, she called out greetings. The hem of her dusky purple wool dress swirled about her tall black heeled boots. She wove her way through the crowd of churchgoers gathered around the front steps. Short of standing awkwardly alone and feeling even more out of place, he shuffled along behind her.

Olly waved at a towheaded little guy. "'Miah."

A year or so older, the child broke into a smile. "Hey, Olly."

"Jeremiah and Olly are best buds." She smiled at the dark-haired man holding the child. "Colton, do you remember Luke Morgan from high school?"

He vaguely recalled Luke—a quiet, kind, serious-minded guy—being a few grades ahead of them. Colton extended his hand.

Luke shook it. "Welcome home."

"Luke is a paramedic with the Truelove Fire Department." Her mouth curved. "But his main claim to fame—"

"Other than being Jeremiah's dad?" Luke's eyebrow quirked.

She laughed. "He also owns a Christmas tree farm."

From the affectionate interaction between Luke and his boy, Colton felt sure the Christmas tree farmer had a great relationship with his son. Exactly what Colton longed for with his child—if only Olly would let him.

"You'll get a military discount on any tree you buy from us next Christmas."

"I appreciate the offer." Colton broadened his chest. "But by Christmas, I won't be in Truelove."

Mollie looked stricken.

Luke's gaze batted back and forth between them. "I see..." Jeremiah squirmed. Luke adjusted his hold. "Better get this one to children's church."

Olly bucked like a bronco. "Down, Mowee. Down."

Lips taut, she jostled Oliver on her hip to distract him. "Thanks so much for that, Colton," she muttered.

He felt like a heel for bursting her bubble of happiness today. But they needed to start laying the groundwork for extricating themselves from the untenable situation of their fake marriage.

Luke turned. "Nice to see you again, Atkinson."

There was a strength on Luke's face—and a peace—he envied. He regretted his brusque words. If he'd been in the market for a friend, Luke might have made a great one.

People trickled inside the sanctuary. Alone on the sidewalk, Mollie turned on Colton so abruptly, the gust of her movement ruffled Olly's hair. The little boy's eyes widened.

"What is wrong with you?" she hissed. "Do you have to be so…so…"

"Honest?" He jammed his hands into his pockets.

"So rude," she huffed. "These people are our friends. His family has been good to us. You are your own worst enemy. You know that, right?"

His lip curled. "People in Truelove are your friends. They've never been mine."

"Luke was making a gesture of friendship." She glowered at him. "If you have no friends here, it's only because you wouldn't let anyone get close to you."

Colton scowled back. "Except you. And why you've put up with me I haven't a clue."

Her expression changed, yet Colton couldn't read it. His lungs constricted.

She turned away, giving him a nice view of her shoulder. A bleakness engulfed him. How had they gotten so off course with each other? He used to know her better than he understood himself.

But it was as he'd feared. The moment they'd broken their self-imposed friends-only pact, everything they'd meant to each other had begun to unravel.

His gut twisted. He'd lost her. They'd lost each other.

She pawed through the diaper bag. "Oh, no."

"What's wrong?"

Refusing to look at him, she made to move past him. "I left my Bible in the truck."

He put his hand on her coat. "Get Olly to his class. I'll get your Bible."

Mollie's eyes flitted to his. "Thank you."

He kept his hand on her arm a few seconds longer. He hated it when they were at odds. "I'm sorry for embarrassing you. Next time I'll be less—"

"Antisocial?"

Colton nodded. "I'll try to be more like Ethan or Luke."

"You never need to be anyone other than yourself." She gazed at him. "I wish you would let people see the Colton I know—charming, sincere, smart, funny, sweet—"

"No guy on the planet wants to be called 'sweet,' Molls."

She chuckled. "I'll meet you inside the church."

A soft breeze blew a tendril of her hair against her cheek. He fought the urge to smooth it out of her face. Under the terms of their pact, touching her hair was inappropriate, of course. But still…

He blew out a breath. "Have fun with Jeremiah and your friends, Olly." He touched his son's shoulder.

"Me not Owee." Throwing off Colton's hand, his son bared his teeth. "Me big, scary bear." Growling, he curled his fingers into claws and swiped at the air.

So much for last night's gains at bath time.

"He has a thing about bears." She set Oliver

down, but kept a tight hold on his hand. "Come on then, my scary little teddy bear."

Gravel crunching underneath his boots, Colton retraced his steps over the footbridge to the parking lot. He retrieved Mollie's black leather Bible lying on the seat. Wheeling, he spotted a steel blue Drake Construction vehicle. Her dad was hunched over the steering wheel.

Somebody ought to check on him. But everyone else had already gone into the service. He hated getting involved in other people's business.

His first inclination was to make a wide berth around the truck and leave the man in peace, but something about Ted's slumped shoulders…

Colton gritted his teeth. "Somebody" was going to have to be him.

At the rap of Colton's knuckles on the window, Ted lifted his head. His face drawn, the older man looked exhausted.

"Everything okay, sir?" Colton called through the glass.

With the push of a button, Ted lowered the window. "I'm fine."

The man looked far from fine.

"Where's Miss Glenda?"

Mollie's father stirred. "At home. She's still not mixing in large crowds, but her best friend, Trudy, who manages the Mason Jar, looks after her on Sunday mornings so I can get to church."

Colton flicked a glance at the building.

"You go on now." Ted motioned. "I'll join you in a moment."

Colton cleared his throat. "Is there anything I can do to help you?"

A smile lifted the man's craggy features. "I appreciate the offer, son. Just got a lot on my mind right now with Glenda's health. Drake Construction is also in the middle of several huge projects." He scrubbed his face with his hand. "Sometimes I need a minute to myself."

Nobody understood a need for privacy more than Colton. Yet it was obvious how much of a toll Glenda's health crisis was taking on Ted. Maybe he and Mollie weren't the only ones keeping secrets.

Was Glenda worse? Were Mollie's parents keeping her mother's real prognosis from her? If anything were to happen to her mother, Mollie would be devastated.

Ted took a breath and released it slowly. "But whatever else is going on, it does my heart good to see you back where you belong."

Colton looked at his boots.

"To see you reunited with your son and Mollie. My girl lights up when you enter a room."

His head snapped up. She did? His heart slammed against his ribs.

"Guess I'll walk with you to the church." Heaving a long sigh, Ted raised the window and pushed open the door. "I try to slip into the pew just as the service starts. I appreciate everyone's concern for Glenda, but…"

"Sometimes dealing with the questions is too much."

Ted nodded. "I feel selfish for wanting a break from the cancer. Glenda doesn't get one."

Colton shook his head. "You're the least selfish person I know. Everybody needs time and space to rest their hearts."

"That's what church does for me. Gives me something else, something better, to focus on." Ted cocked his head. "You got smarter while you were overseas."

Colton laughed. "'Bout time, right?" They grinned at each other.

Shoulder to shoulder, they headed toward the sanctuary. Strains of music floated out from the wooden doors. Inside, Mollie sat alone in a pew halfway down the carpeted aisle. She'd probably been wondering where he'd gotten to. Her features lifted as soon as she saw them. She scooted over to give them room.

He hung back to allow her father to slide in, but the older man motioned him forward. As was only proper, Colton supposed, given he was Mollie's husband.

Flushing, he kept his head down as he moved into the pew. Some husband. He'd been deployed mere hours after their courthouse wedding. It took a mental adjustment to think of himself as Mollie's husband. But that was what he was—at least on paper.

Sitting down, he gripped his jean-clad thighs.

This close to her, he couldn't fail to notice the citrusy scent of her shampoo.

She touched his hand. "Everything okay?" She shifted her focus beyond him to her father.

If her parents were hiding facts in an effort to spare her, the ruse wasn't as effective as the Drakes probably believed.

"What is it?" she whispered.

If she lost her mom after losing Olly… He wasn't sure Mollie could survive two such losses.

People rose from their places in the pews, hymnals clutched in their hands. He stood, too. She snagged his arm. "Colton…"

The music swelled.

He leaned close, and his mouth brushed the lock of hair against her ear. As silky as he'd always supposed. His heart skipped a beat. "Nothing for you to worry about, Molls."

His breath sent the rebellious tendril of hair dangling against her earlobe. A smile played about her lips.

Suddenly, it struck him how kissable those lips of hers were. Another inappropriate revelation given their current whereabouts. Not to mention their friends-only vow.

Although that wasn't the only vow they'd taken. A lump settled at the base of his throat. This wasn't going to—couldn't—end well.

Mollie, what have we done?

Chapter Four

Colton didn't have much experience with church. He'd never attended an Easter service before. As a teenager, he went a couple of times to the youth group with Mollie.

Today, not wanting to do the wrong thing, he stood when she stood. He sat when she sat.

Huge hand-hewn beams soared above his head. Stained glass windows lined the exterior walls. A white cloth was draped over the large wooden cross sitting on the altar.

Colton recognized former high school classmates and people from the Easter egg hunt. Across the aisle, Ethan, Amber and their girls were seated together. A few pews ahead, Sam Gibson and his wife, Lila, sat with their little girl.

With their significant others, the matchmakers occupied an entire pew near the front.

A guitar in hand, a familiar-looking petite blonde walked onto the platform. Fingering the chords, she began to sing, and he sat up a bit straighter. Her voice was compelling and strong.

"Is that Shayla Coggins?" he whispered to Mollie.

Shayla hailed from the same dead-end mountain hollow as him. Sam Gibson, too.

But the Coggins were ne'er-do-wells, renowned for their penchant for the wrong side of the law. He'd always felt sorry for her. Colton had had a rough childhood, but Shayla'd had it worse.

"She's Shayla Morgan now. Jeremiah's mom and Luke's wife."

"*The* Shayla Morgan?" he rasped. "With the hit single topping the country music charts?"

Mollie turned toward the platform. "Truelove's very own songbird."

Opposite the Gibsons, Luke perched on the edge of the pew, his face rapt and adoring.

Shayla had an extraordinary talent. Despite not being musical, Colton couldn't help but become caught up in the song and the beauty of her voice. Closing her eyes, she sang about a love greater than any other love.

He peered at Mollie. Her face shone, as did her dad's. A look of hope had replaced the weary despair Colton had glimpsed in the parking lot.

When Shayla finished, the last note hung clear and pure, hovering in the rafters over everyone like a blessing. She joined her husband.

Reverend Bryant, a thin scholarly man with a kind face, got behind the pulpit. "He is risen."

The congregation responded in one accord. "He is risen indeed."

Hope. Joy. Peace. The sermon was short, but powerful.

Colton had heard the resurrection story before. But this time—maybe because of where he'd spent the last months amid so much death and destruction—the real significance of it struck him.

After a benediction, the organ sounded. Everyone rose. He took a final look at the wooden cross on the altar. Later, he'd like to further ponder everything he'd heard today.

Exchanging Easter greetings with other churchgoers, Mollie milled about the sanctuary. Laughing, happy children darted out the open doors to the beckoning sunshine. He was thankful Olly had this place in his life thus far. He wanted to do better by his son than his parents had done by him. Maybe once he and Oliver were settled, he could find a church for the both of them.

What shocked Colton to his core, though, was how many people stopped to talk with him. Had Mollie been right about the chip on his shoulder keeping Truelove at arm's length?

They welcomed him home. Wished him well in his future endeavors, which most assumed would be spent in Truelove. To his consternation, they also congratulated him and Mollie on their marriage.

"Glenda and Ted's girl is a real keeper," one old-timer told him.

"She's the best," another Truelover declared.

Mollie blushed to the roots of her hair.

Colton put his arm around her slim waist. "Yes. She is." The absolute best.

He kept an eye on the matchmakers, lest he find

himself cornered. Their capacity for mischief and mayhem was not to be discounted. Even on Easter Sunday.

With ErmaJean bustling toward them, he was contemplating a hasty retreat to the nearest exit when Ted's phone buzzed. Stepping aside, Mollie's father took the call.

A few seconds later, he groaned. "Oh, no."

Mollie went rigid. "Daddy?"

He clutched the cell to his ear. "I'm on my way."

She seized his arm. "What's happened?"

Hand shaking, Ted clicked off the phone. "Trudy says your mom has taken a turn for the worse. I—I need to get home..." His gaze took in the emptying sanctuary. Everyone around them had gone stock-still.

Mollie put her hand to her throat. "What's wrong with Mom?"

A distinguished-looking man about her father's age, who'd been sitting with Luke's family, stepped forward. "Ted, how about I drive you home and take a look at Glenda?"

Ted's eyes were slightly glazed. "Thank you, Dr. Jernigan." He spun around. "Mollie girl?"

"I'm here, Daddy. Colton?"

The look on her face gutted him. He knew it was taking everything in her to not fall apart. He wished with all his heart he could make it so she didn't have to go through this with her mom.

Colton took hold of her hand. "We're both here,

sir." He exchanged a quick glance with Mollie. "We'll follow you and the doctor."

Mollie blinked rapidly. "Just as soon as we get Olly from the nursery."

Shayla touched her shoulder. "Luke's heading over with the ambulance crew in case they're needed. I can take Olly home with me. After lunch, he and Jeremiah can play."

As she lost her struggle to not give in to tears, Mollie's eyes overflowed. "Thank you. He loves playing at the tree farm."

Shayla hugged her. "We love having Olly. My sisters-in-law will probably compete to see who can spoil him the most."

The doctor and Ted set off.

Shayla gave Colton a shy smile. "I'm sorry we had to meet again under such circumstances."

He cleared his throat. "Thank you for offering to take care of Olly."

"That's what friends are for, right?" She gave Mollie another hug. "Don't worry about rushing back. We'll see you when we see you."

She hurried toward the education building. He found himself and Mollie encircled by the matchmakers.

GeorgeAnne's mouth pursed. "We couldn't help but overhear."

ErmaJean's features crumpled. "Glenda's fought so long and so hard," she whispered. The seventysomething older woman looked as fragile as he ever recalled seeing her.

IdaLee slipped her arm around her dear friend. “We’re going to sit down right now and pray.”

“Thank you.” Mollie kissed her aunt EJ’s cheek. “I’ll keep you updated.”

Colton steered her toward the door. Behind him, a soft murmur of voices rose as they lifted Mollie’s mom in prayer.

That was the thing about the matchmakers. Interfering, meddling busybodies they might be, but they loved their neighbors through every crisis, large or small. Community, faith and prayer would get the Drakes through this latest setback.

He and Mollie hurried over the footbridge to the nearly vacant parking lot. At the sight of her dad’s abandoned vehicle, he resolved to retrieve it later.

After helping Mollie into the truck, he rounded the hood to get behind the wheel.

She struggled with her seat belt. “I can’t… It won’t—”

“Let me.” Reaching, he took the buckle from her and clicked it into place. “There.”

She heaved a sigh. “What if Mom—”

“I know you’re scared.” He squeezed her hand. “But you mustn’t think the worst.”

Her mouth wobbled, but she nodded.

At the midcentury modern brick house where Mollie had grown up, he pulled in between a hunter-green Subaru and a parked ambulance.

She thrust open the door. “Russell Jernigan is also Olly’s pediatrician.” She hopped out.

The doctor met them on the porch in his shirtsleeves.

"Is she—" Mollie staggered. Colton put a bracing hand on her back. "My mom…"

"She's dehydrated." The fiftysomething doctor held the door for them. "But I think she's going to be all right."

Mollie stumbled inside. "Where's my dad?"

"Ted's with her now." The doctor gestured toward the end of the hall. "I called her oncologist. Luke is inserting an IV drip line to replace the fluids she's lost."

Inside the master bedroom, Glenda lay on the bed, propped against the pillows.

Mollie went straight to her mother's side. "Mom?"

Glenda reached for her daughter. Sinking onto the mattress, Mollie gripped her hand. Glenda threw Colton a weak smile. "Sorry to ruin everyone's Easter."

Ted sat slumped in a nearby armchair.

Colton stood by Mollie's dad. "You didn't ruin anything, Miss Glenda."

Dr. Jernigan reslung a stethoscope around his neck. "Reheated dinners are an occupational hazard in health care."

Trudy McKendry waggled her fingers at him. "Long time no see, Colton Atkinson." Larger-than-life with her platinum blond hair and bright red lipstick, she winked at him. "Last time our paths crossed, you ordered a Rock Your World milkshake for yourself and a Red Velvet Cake milkshake for your future wife."

"And where there was one, there was always the other." Glenda's green eyes crinkled at the corners. "I couldn't be happier about the way things have turned out."

He swallowed past the boulder in his throat.

Mollie turned toward Dr. Jernigan. "You're sure she's going to be okay?"

"Dehydration is a common and unfortunate side effect of chemo." The doc slipped his arms into his coat. "I think two bags of saline should do the trick. I'll return in a few hours to remove the IV."

Glenda made a motion. "I hate for you to—"

"It's no bother. Your oncologist wants to see you and your husband at her office tomorrow morning so she can do a more thorough assessment."

Glenda's mouth downturned. "Must we go again so soon?" She cast a hopeful look at the doctor. "I'm already feeling perkier."

Ted leaned forward, his elbows on his knees. "Perky or not, we'll do whatever the doctors think is best."

A line formed between her brows. "But you have that meeting..."

Ted smoothed a strand of hair off his wife's forehead. "I'll make it work. You concentrate on regaining your strength."

Soon after, the doctor and Luke left Trudy to monitor the drip line. Colton offered to drive Ted to retrieve his truck. Gazing out the window on the drive over, Mollie's father remained quiet.

His heart went out to Ted, who was determined to do his best for his wife but overwhelmed with business responsibilities.

When they pulled into the church parking lot, Ted stirred. "I don't know what plans you've made for future employment in Truelove."

Colton dropped his gaze.

Ted scrubbed the back of his neck. "You may have a terrific job lined up, starting tomorrow."

Not in Truelove he didn't.

Colton took a breath. "I don't have anything lined up yet. Why?"

"Would you consider coming alongside me and acting as a foreman on my current projects?"

Colton gaped at him. "What?"

"You worked summers with me."

"As a laborer," Colton pointed out. "Not as a foreman. I don't have a contractor's license."

"I need someone I trust who can keep the subcontractors on schedule and the project moving forward."

"For how long, Mr. Ted?"

"Just until I can get Glenda's health stabilized, I promise." Ted grimaced. "You don't know how it pains me to impose on you and Mollie."

Ted was a proud man. He would hate being beholden to anyone. He'd been good to Colton. It was time to try to return the favor.

"You're not imposing." Then he voiced something he never believed he'd ever have occasion to say. "That's what families are for. To help one another." Colton's gaze found his. "For as long as you need me."

Ted thanked him and went over a few pressing details for Monday morning, including a visit by a building inspector.

Colton followed Ted's truck to the Drake residence.

Mollie came out. "Mom's resting, Daddy. Trudy said for you not even to think about arguing, but she's staying the night to look after Mom."

Ted sighed. "What would we do without friends?" He smiled at Colton. "And family." Her father went inside the house.

Colton took her hand. "How can I help you?"

She glanced at his hand on hers. "Being here is the best thing you can do for me." An artery pulsed in the hollow of her throat.

He felt a sudden and inexplicable urge to hold her, to comfort her, to soothe away the fears clouding her eyes, to lov—

No. That wasn't their deal. But as for everything else…

"I'm not going anywhere, Molls."

And because they were nothing if not honest with each other, he amended his statement. "Not for a while anyway."

Before he could talk himself out of it, because he could no longer deny the need to comfort her, he tugged her close and held her in his arms.

She leaned her head against his shoulder. "I miss Olly."

In that moment, something sweet and right flooded through him. He couldn't imagine anywhere on earth he'd rather be than with her.

Don't think about next week. Or next month. Or next year. Just enjoy now.

Once he and Olly left, nothing would—could—ever be the same. Not for him and Mollie.

He brushed his lips across the top of her head. "Let's go get our boy."

The next morning, Mollie had a pot of coffee ready by the time Colton staggered into the kitchen. With Colton working for her dad and traveling to jobsites, her mornings would start earlier than usual.

He took a sip from the mug she handed him. "You are a lifesaver."

Colton gave her a crooked smile. Her knees went wobbly.

In his booster seat, Olly clanged his spoon against his bowl.

Colton took another sip. "Good morning to you, too, Oliver."

Olly gave him a less-than-friendly look before shoveling oatmeal into his mouth.

Colton shrugged. "Worth a try."

"Don't get discouraged. It's early days yet." She stirred the pot on the stove. "Would you like some oatmeal before you leave?"

Wrapping his hands around the mug, he leaned against the counter. "Not sure I can. Big day, lots to do. Tons of projects to get caught up on."

"You should eat something. To keep up your strength." She scooped oatmeal into a bowl. "Dad has faith you can handle this."

He pulled out a chair next to Oliver. "I hope his faith isn't misplaced."

She put the bowl in front of him. "It isn't." She motioned to small bowls of nuts, berries and brown sugar on the lazy Susan in the middle of the table. "Fix it however you like. The jug contains cream."

He helped himself to the brown sugar, poured a smidgen of cream over his oatmeal, then topped off the hot cereal with a few blueberries.

She sat beside him with her own bowl. "Daddy puts blueberries in his breakfast just like you, Olly."

For about two seconds, breakfast was everything she'd dreamed of with two of her favorite guys in the world.

But making a face, Oliver picked a blueberry out of his bowl. He pinched the blueberry between his thumb and forefinger and flicked it at the lazy Susan.

She gasped. "Oliver Edward Atkinson!"

With a marked disdain in his cherubic blue eyes, Olly flicked a blueberry at Colton.

She jumped to her feet. Colton made a strangled sound in the back of his throat.

"Don't you dare laugh. This isn't funny." She

wagged her finger. "He can't be allowed to get away with such outrageous behavior."

"You're right." Choking off another laugh, Colton put his hand over his mouth. "Kind of have to admire his determination not to like me, though. Once he commits to a course of action, he isn't easily deterred, is he?" He chuckled. "Says a lot about his strength of character and tenacity."

She snorted. "Says more about his pigheadedness." She took the bowl away from Oliver.

The child made a vain attempt to grab it. But she was quicker.

She held it out of his reach. "Until you can eat your breakfast like a big boy, I'll have to feed you like Miss AnnaBeth feeds baby Violet."

Oliver scowled. "Not a baby." His lips poked out.

She sniffed. "Then stop acting like one."

Colton stirred his cereal. "Baby Violet who?"

"You met AnnaBeth at church yesterday. The tall, beautiful redhead."

"Sounds like you, except for the tall part."

For a second, Mollie blinked at him.

Unsure if she should take offense or be flattered at the backhanded compliment, she buried her blush by taking a sip of coffee. "AnnaBeth and her husband, Jonas Stone, own the dude ranch outside town. Their daughter, Violet, isn't quite a year old. For some reason, Oliver is fascinated with her." She glanced at the little boy. "It's not like Olly to act up like this. I don't know what's gotten into him."

With a pointed look aimed at the tiny rebel in the

booster seat, Colton shoved a spoonful of oatmeal into his mouth. "Yum."

Oliver scowled.

She opened her hands. "What are you doing?"

"After the bathtub incident, I'm rethinking the soft and cuddly approach."

She rolled her eyes. "In favor of a spitting contest?"

Oliver's gaze jerked to hers.

She held up her hand. "Don't go there." She frowned at them. "Either of you."

It didn't take a child psychologist to figure out Olly felt confused by his father's sudden appearance. Maybe on an instinctive level, the child worried that Colton would take Mollie away from him. Except it was the other way around. Colton would be taking him away from her.

She drooped in her chair.

"Me sorry, Mowee." Olly held out his hand to her. "Me eat wike big boy. Pwease?"

She scanned his face to gauge his sincerity. After a moment, she set the bowl in front of him. "Hard to resist those puppy dog eyes of his," she grumbled. "Let's try this again, shall we, Oliver?"

"You don't give yourself enough credit. You do a good job with him."

She watched to make sure Olly made good on his promise to eat responsibly. "Some people have to learn everything the hard way. Sound familiar?"

He cocked his head. "Why do I get the feeling I've just been slurred?"

"If the hard hat fits…"

He threw her a lopsided smile. "Like father, like son."

She snorted. "Clearly a case of nature versus nurture."

His lips twitched. "Clearly." He slid back his chair. "I better get going."

She rose. "I put together a lunch for you."

He rinsed his bowl and coffee cup in the sink. "You didn't have to do that. You must have gotten up at the crack of dawn to prepare breakfast and lunch."

"Your son likes to get up with the birds. I was up anyway." She handed him a brown paper bag. "Sandwich. Chips. Cookies."

"Thanks." He leaned his hip against the island. "Not sure what time I'll make it back tonight."

"Not a problem." She fluttered her hand. "I'm the daughter of a contractor, remember? We'll see you when we see you. I'll keep a plate warm for you."

"Much appreciated." He lingered in the doorway, as if he wasn't ready to say goodbye. "What does your day look like, Molls?"

"I'll be at the salon. Olly attends a Mother's Morning Out program at the preschool. Aunt EJ picks him up from there. Feeds him lunch and looks after him until I get home."

She opened the fridge and handed Colton a cold bottle of water. "I try not to schedule any clients after three o'clock. Olly's usually just waking up from his nap. I spend the rest of the afternoon with him until supper."

"Oliver's blessed to have you in his life." His gaze drifted to her. "Me, too."

She beheld a certain wistfulness in his features. And affection. Yet it pained her to contemplate his affection might no longer be enough for her.

"I'm the blessed one." She gave him a quick hug and just as quickly pulled away. "No more stalling. It's going to be a fabulously fantastic, marvelously wonderful kind of day."

Colton laughed. "Little Miss Sunshine. Always the optimist. How do you keep such a positive outlook?"

"Hope springs eternal." She patted his arm. "You ought to try it some time."

Shrugging into a jacket, he threw her a cheeky grin. "Maybe I will. Olly?" He paused. "Daddy loves you. I'll see you later, alligator."

Oliver crinkled his nose. "Me not a-wee-gator."

Colton waved at his son. "After a while, crocodile."

"Me not crwoc," the little boy called after his father.

But a small smile played about Oliver's mouth. Just before he popped a blueberry into it.

Raising her eyes to the ceiling, she shook her head. Like father, like son indeed. Contrary. Muleheaded. Totally exasperating.

She gripped the edge of the porcelain sink.

How would she ever live without them?

Chapter Five

That morning at Hair Raisers, Mollie checked her phone often. But she was in the middle of rolling Dorothy Summerfield's silvery hair when her phone rang.

Pink roller in hand, she checked her cell on the black Formica countertop. "It's my dad," she told the octogenarian's reflection in the wall mirror.

Sitting in the black swivel chair, the pink-caped Dorothy motioned. "You should take that." Now living in a fancy retirement community with her new husband, the retired cattle matriarch still traveled once a month to Truelove for a shampoo and set.

Mollie's phone continued to ring.

"I don't usually take calls when I'm with a client, Miss Dot."

"Howard is having breakfast with my grandson, Clay. I'm in no hurry. Find out what's going on with your mother."

Mollie caught the phone on the last ring before it routed to voice mail. "Daddy?" She moved to the supply room for more privacy. "Where are you?"

He chuckled. "Hello and good morning to you, too, Mollie girl."

In her stomach, the hard, tight coil of fear she'd felt since church yesterday unfurled a notch. He was in a good mood. Maybe the news wasn't terrible.

"Your mother and I just returned home."

"What did the doctor say?"

"Same thing Dr. Jernigan told us. Her dehydration triggered the spell. The saline drip set her right. Her oncologist ordered a follow-up scan to determine if the treatments did their job to slow or stop the cancer's progress."

She clutched the phone. "Does that mean Mom could be cancer-free?"

"The scan could also show the cancer is merely stable—neither worse nor better. Or, that she's in partial remission."

She pressed the phone to her ear. "What's the worst-case scenario?"

"That the cancer has progressed. Grown or spread." He sighed. "Metastasized."

Closing her eyes, she leaned against the wall. If "cancer" was the scariest word in the world, "metastasized" came a close second.

"But we're believing in God for complete remission. Mom said to tell you to keep the faith."

Hot tears pricked at her eyelids. "I'll try," she whispered. "When is the scan?"

"In a few weeks." Her father cleared his throat. "In the meantime, we need to build up her strength and stamina. Glorieta Ferguson brought her another nutrition-packed meal to tempt your mom's appetite."

Everyone had been so kind. Glorieta, the barbecue queen of North Carolina and Kara MacKenzie's adoptive mom, had created weekly meals for Mollie's mom, designed to boost the cancer patient's embattled immune system.

Mollie swallowed. "What's on today's menu?"

"Now that she's past the nausea, salmon and sweet potatoes."

"You're making me hungry."

"She brought enough for me, too." He laughed. "Glorieta's going to stay with her for a few hours while I head over to the jobsite to touch base with Colton."

Mollie straightened. "Was there a problem?" She'd been praying for Colton's first day on the job.

"Nope. I talked to him before we left the clinic. He handled the inspection like a pro. The project passed with flying colors. Just thought I'd check on him. Make sure he's not feeling overwhelmed."

"Because you know how that feels, don't you, Daddy?"

"Colton's an answer to our prayers. No one but God will ever know how much it meant for me to be able to take care of your mom today."

She worried about her dad. There was more salt than pepper in his hair these days. The lines on his face had become more pronounced. Studies were clear about the impact cancer exacted on a patient's loved ones.

Running his company while caring for his beloved wife had taken a toll. He felt a heavy responsibility to provide a livelihood for the people who worked for him, so they could take care of their families.

"Any words you want me to pass on when I see your bridegroom, Mollie girl?"

She blushed. Bridegroom in name only. "Uh… I don't know."

Her dad laughed. "How 'bout I just tell him you're thinking of him?"

Ever and always.

Mollie suddenly recalled Miss Dot, waiting for her hair to be rolled. "I gotta go, Daddy. Talk to you soon."

She found Dorothy chatting with Mollie's next appointment—Wilda Arledge, the sixtysomething mother of Truelove's police chief.

Mollie grabbed the spray bottle and spritzed water on the older woman's head to dampen her hair again. "I'm running behind today, Miss Wilda."

"No worries. I'm early." Wilda fluttered her hand. "Long as I'm done by the time school lets out. I promised my grandsons I'd pick them up at car pool."

Mollie reached for another roller. "That's doable." Using the pointy end of a comb, she separated a small section of Dorothy's hair, gave it a quick roll around the curler and secured it in place. "I'm sorry for keeping you waiting, Miss Dot."

Dorothy gave Mollie a serene smile. "Wilda and I enjoyed catching up with each other."

Trim and attractive, Wilda sat down at the nearby hooded dryer chair. "What's the latest report from the doctor?"

While she rolled the rest of Dorothy's hair, she gave them an update.

Dorothy patted her arm. "We'll let the prayer chain know to pray the cancer is gone."

"Thank you." She helped Dorothy out of the chair. "Let's get you under the hood."

Dorothy and Wilda exchanged places. Mollie lowered the hood, set the timer and handed the older woman a glossy travel magazine.

She led Wilda to the shampoo chair at the sink. Mollie gently lowered the back of the chair. "Scooch closer, Miss Wilda."

Wilda wriggled until her neck was in the proper position. "What's the latest on Truelove's returning hero and my favorite hairdresser?"

Suppressing the urge to sigh, she turned on the faucet and tested the water temperature. She and Colton would remain big news on the Truelove grapevine until another hapless pair captured the matchmakers' attention.

The matchmakers meant well. Really. They did. She was almost sure of it.

"We're concentrating on getting life back to normal, Miss Wilda."

"There's no arguing with success." Wilda grinned. "Nor with the matchmakers."

Several years ago, Wilda Hollingsworth and Tom Arledge had been the objects of a successful matchmaking project. So successful, her son and Tom's daughter ended up falling in love and marrying, too.

"Another pair bites the dust." Wilda giggled. "What does that bring the matchmakers' total count to now?"

She had no idea. But their situation wasn't anything like what Wilda imagined.

Mollie ran a stream of water over Wilda's hair. It hadn't been the matchmakers who paired her and Colton but, rather, Colton's sudden deployment.

Yet apparently the matchmakers aimed to take full credit for another Made-in-Truelove love match.

Wilda caught hold of her hand on the spray nozzle. "The matchmakers will make sure you and that handsome hunk of yours make up for lost time." She chuckled. "All you've got to do is sit back and enjoy the ride."

A sentiment less comforting than Wilda probably supposed. Secrets had a way of sucking the joy out of a situation.

That evening, Colton came home tired, but a new sense of satisfaction that hadn't been there that morning settled over him.

She smiled. "You had a good day."

He hung his jacket in the foyer closet. "I had a great teacher."

"Daddy was singing your praises."

"We make a great team. I love working with him again."

"It's a mutual-admiration society. He loves spending time with you. Always has." She winked. "If I didn't know better, I'd say you married me because of my dad."

"At last, the truth comes out." He threw her a teasing, lopsided smile, setting butterflies fluttering inside her chest. "Besides Olly, your parents are my favorite people in the world."

"Hey." She planted her hands on her hips. "What am I? Chopped liver?"

Colton's lips quirked. "You are in a category all by yourself."

"Would that be a good kind of category or not?"

"Definitely good." He followed her into the kitchen. "Hey, son." He went to the sink to wash his hands.

In his booster seat, Oliver grunted.

Colton shook his head. "Not much of a mutual-admiration society here."

After dinner, she wrangled Colton into reading Oliver his nightly bedtime story. He pulled one of the books from the basket in the living room.

Since Oliver refused to sit in his father's lap, she held the little boy while they listened to the story. Olly's soft curls smelled of baby shampoo.

As he read, Colton did a good job of showing them the illustrations. Arms folded across his tiny pj's, Oliver remained unmoved by Colton's rendition of the plucky little West Highland white terrier.

Reaching the end, Colton closed the book and threw her a long-suffering look.

"It'll get better," she promised for the umpteenth time.

She set Olly on his feet. The kid could win awards for Most Stubborn Boy of All Time. "His favorite stories involve bears. Try one of those next time."

Over the next few days, Mollie integrated Colton into Oliver's daily routine as best as she could. They had breakfast together every morning before Colton joined her father at the jobsite. To her relief, no more blueberry-throwing incidents occurred.

By Friday, she'd begun to believe they'd dodged the Double Name Club bullet. There'd been no talk from the matchmakers about recreating any so-called matrimonial milestones.

Midmorning during a lull between clients at the salon, she tidied the reception area. Martha Alice Breckenridge was due soon for her weekly shampoo and set. Mollie had tried to maintain her mom's well-earned reputation with their clientele.

With a few minutes to spare, she stood at the large picture window overlooking the town square. She never tired of the view of Truelove. Once upon a lifetime ago, she'd gone to the state capital in the flatlands to attend beauty school, but she'd grown tired of the indifferent anonymity of the big city. A mountain girl at heart, she'd yearned for the slower pace of life. The simplicity and goodness of small things.

She'd been on the verge of returning to Truelove when Erin, Oliver's mother, died after giving birth to him. Mollie had fallen in love with the infant at first sight. As children, she and Colton had been everything to each other. She would have done anything to help him. And she did.

Including marrying him when his combat brigade received no-notice deployment orders and he found himself with no family to take care of his infant son.

The bell over the door jangled. She turned from her contemplations to smile at Martha Alice. However, the elegant older woman wasn't alone. The smile froze on Mollie's face.

Clipboard under her arm, GeorgeAnne stormed into the salon.

"Great news," the Iron Lady of Truelove declared. "Took a while to ensure the details were in place, but tonight we're ready to help you and Colton celebrate the sweetheart Valentine's Day you missed."

"Tonight?" she squeaked.

GeorgeAnne gave her a decisive nod. "Tonight."

"Miss GeorgeAnne—"

"No need to thank me." GeorgeAnne lifted an imperious hand. "It's the least we can do for Truelove's hometown hero."

"But Olly—"

"Oliver will have the time of his life at Amber's. We're bringing the festivities to your house."

Martha Alice patted her handbag. "I have my instructions for the flowers."

"Right." GeorgeAnne checked off an item on her clipboard. "We'll supply the food and the ambience…"

Ambience?

"…Mollie and Colton will supply the romance."

The two older ladies tittered. A flush crept from beneath Mollie's collar.

"You don't need to worry about a thing, except getting properly reacquainted with your husband. Reacquainted. Get it?" GeorgeAnne cackled. "Wink. Wink."

The Double Name Club president proceeded to actually wink. Martha Alice's eyes twinkled. Like a guppy gasping on air, Mollie's mouth opened and closed.

GeorgeAnne cocked her head. "You still keep your extra house key under the planter on the porch?"

In a small town like Truelove, the location of spare keys was rarely a mystery.

She tensed. "Yesssss…"

GeorgeAnne propped her hands on her bony hips. "The girls and I will get right to work transforming your house."

"No!" Mollie's eyes went deer-in-the-headlights wide. "You can't go in there."

How many newlyweds had separate bedrooms?

"Why not?"

"Because..." Mollie racked her brain for a plausible-sounding excuse. Otherwise, the truth of her fake marriage would be all over Truelove within the hour. "Ummmm...my house... I—I haven't had a chance to tidy up..."

The two ladies stared at her.

"Don't get your curlers in a wad." GeorgeAnne wagged a finger. "No one will mind the mess."

"I mind..." She considered making a wild dash home and tossing Colton's belongings into her bedroom. But with her day booked solid, there was no way she could get over there to hide the evidence.

"Here's an idea." Mollie painted a bright smile on her face. "What about postponing until tomorrow?"

"I had no idea you were so house-proud." GeorgeAnne lifted her chin. "But we can't postpone. The wheels are already in motion."

Mollie wrung her hands. "I haven't had a chance to straighten the bedroom."

Of course, she meant "bedrooms" in the plural.

"The Double Name Club will not violate your privacy." GeorgeAnne waved away her concerns. "We intend to confine our efforts to the public areas of the house in the kitchen and living room."

Mollie gnawed at her lip. "It's been a long week. Colton probably would rather have a laid-back evening at home with dinner in front of the TV."

GeorgeAnne's pencil-thin eyebrow rose. "You young people need to learn how to have a good time, which is why... Wait for it..." The matchmaker smirked. "Tonight's Valentine theme is fun-due."

"You mean fondue?"

"I mean fun-due," GeorgeAnne growled. "Stop taking yourselves so seriously and live a little."

"Colton—"

"Don't worry your pretty head about that man of yours." GeorgeAnne yanked open the door, setting off a flurry of jangling bells. "I'm on my way to the construction site to let him know what time he'll need to knock off work today."

Swamped with the project, he was going to have a fit.

As if reading her mind—God forbid—GeorgeAnne sniffed. "It's the weekend." Her mouth flattened. "An hour or two early won't make or break the schedule. After your last customer, you head home and concentrate on getting yourself gussied up. See you later."

The matchmaker blew out of the hair salon like a tropical wind at full throttle. Mollie gazed bleakly after her.

"It'll be fun." Martha Alice put a delicate hand to the pearls resting against her throat. "I think."

The rest of the afternoon was a blur. When the last customer departed, Mollie locked the door behind them. The upcoming fondue party was the talk of the town.

She'd received a steady stream of well-wishes for a wonderful evening from her mom and just about everyone else in Truelove.

Yet from Colton, there'd been not so much as a peep. Which wasn't necessarily unusual. But she thought she would have heard something from him. Between haircuts and highlighting jobs, she'd fretted.

Her inability to tell the truth about their marriage had boxed him into playing along with this absurd matchmaking game. He probably was irate beyond words. Now he was being forced to pretend to woo his fake Valentine's sweetheart.

The evening had the makings of a disaster.

A bevy of vehicles was parked outside her house, including Aunt EJ's car and several others.

Lila met her at the door with strict instructions to head straight to her bedroom, looking neither to the left nor to the right on her way.

With Oliver spending the evening with Amber and her kids, it felt strange to have time to herself. Exiled to her bedroom, she caught the scraping sound of furniture being moved in the living room. From the kitchen came the clink of tinkling glasses and cutlery.

About five o'clock, she heard Colton's truck pull into the driveway. Her stomach knotted. A few minutes later, the front door opened and closed. Her heart thumped.

There was a murmur of low voices. He, too, must have been met by one of the Double Name Club members or their honorary associates. She followed the sound of his tread along the hallway to the guest room. Then a worrying silence prevailed.

In an effort to keep busy, she took special care with her hair and makeup. She scrounged through her not-so-sizable wardrobe for something appropriate for the occasion.

Valentine's in April called for clothing a bit more splendid than the usual T-shirt and jeans she wore at the salon. With Olly in her life, it had been a long time since she had any use for fancy evening attire.

She came upon a dress hanging in the back of the closet she'd forgotten she owned. A dress she'd never worn. She put it on before she could talk herself out of it.

It was a light, soft red cotton with small white floral motifs and a V-neckline. The color checked the Valentine's box. Bell sleeves fell to just above her elbow. The hem ended slightly north of her knees.

And there were pockets. She smiled. She loved a dress with pockets. She slipped her feet into a pair of strappy white high-heeled sandals.

As she slowly turned, the dress flared around her legs. She took a critical gander at herself in the full-length mirror. The high heels lengthened her legs and gave her calves a nice shape. She liked the way the dress made her feel. Casual and at the same time, a tad flirty.

Mollie's cheeks heated. She reminded herself—sternly—the evening was only about the optics. None of this was real. She and Colton weren't a real couple.

Unable to resist, she peeked over her shoulder at

her reflection. If she did say so herself, the dress looked good on her. Real question—what would Colton think?

She frowned at her reflection. As if Colton's opinion mattered. She sank onto the edge of the mattress.

Who was she kidding? It mattered. A lot. To her.

Not used to seeing her dolled up, he'd probably take one look at her and burst out laughing.

She and Colton had never spent a Valentine's together. Butterflies swirled in her belly. Like it was their first date. Which it kind of was.

Only no one knew that, except for her and Colton.

She was being silly. Ridiculous. Abruptly, she rose.

They would have to playact their way through whatever romantic scenario the matchmakers had set up for them. Long enough to make it look real and placate the old women.

Mollie squared her shoulders. Then they would collect Oliver from Amber's and return to their friendship-only, romance-free normal relationship.

She tucked and untucked the same strand of hair behind her ear. At present, their relationship was anything but normal.

"Mollie! Colton!" Aunt EJ called. "You can come out now."

She threw another anxious look at the mirror, but it was too late to change. "Ready or not," she whispered.

Mostly not.

In the foyer, Aunt EJ's face crinkled into a broad smile. "Don't you look a treat, honey bun."

The door to the guest bedroom squeaked open, and for a moment, sudden quaking terror ran through her. She should have warned Colton. Aunt EJ would know their marriage wasn't real.

But Aunt EJ's smile only broadened further. "Doesn't your bride look a treat for your belated Valentine's date, Colton?"

Mollie winced.

"A real treat," he said.

She looked at him. He didn't clean up too badly himself. Way to wow.

The button-down shirt emphasized his broad shoulders and tapered at his trim waist. The color brought out the blue in his eyes. Instead of his usual jeans, he wore a pair of gray trousers.

"I'll leave you to enjoy your *fun*-due evening." Aunt EJ chuckled at her own joke. "It never gets old, does it?" Edging toward the door, she prattled on. "Make sure you follow the instructions on the table."

Instructions?

"GeorgeAnne and IdaLee are waiting for me in the car. You can thank us later. Bye now." With a flutter of her fingers, she was gone, closing the door behind her with a click.

The silence draped over them like a mantle. Her heart pounded in her chest. The awkwardness of the moment stretched taut between them.

Mollie wished the floor would open up and swallow her. Colton probably couldn't wait to leave Truelove and its peculiar inhabitants in the dust for good. And who could blame him?

She had to do something—anything—to make this better. Stepping to the door, she threw the bolt in place. It would be just like the meddling trio to pop in to survey their handiwork in action.

Turning sharply on her heel, she faced him. The dress—for the love of hair spray, why had she ever believed this dress was a good idea?—whirled around her legs.

His eyes flickered.

"'Thanks' isn't what will spring to my lips when I see Aunt EJ next." She pressed her palms against the panel of the door. "But they're gone. We're alone. We don't have to go along with anything they've concocted."

He shrugged. "They went to a lot of trouble because they care about us."

She threw out her hands. "You can't seriously want to follow through with this 'date.'" She scrunched her nose.

He crossed his arms over his chest. "Why not?"

She despised herself for noticing the ripple of muscle under his shirt. "We're friends. We're not—"

"It seems a shame to waste the food." Dropping his arms, he sniffed the air. "I'm starving. It smells great."

For the first time, she got a good look at the

changes the matchmaker cupids had wrought on her house.

The living room furniture had been pushed against the walls, except for the coffee table still sitting in the middle of the rug. Throw pillows were scattered around the table, doubling as seating. Lighted pillar candles adorned nearly every conceivable surface. A banner with pink-and-red paper hearts was strung across the mantel, reading *Love, Laughter and Happily-Ever-After.*

A vase of pink tulips—her favorite—occupied a prominent spot on the coffee table. A spirit lamp underneath a large fondue pot kept the melted contents warm. Divided plates contained savory samplings to complement the cheese—chunks of bread, apple slices, quartered red potatoes, an assortment of green veggies, salami and meatballs.

Despite her misgivings about the entire fiasco, she couldn't help but be impressed.

Colton gave a low whistle. "How did the Double Name Club manage to put together such a sophisticated spread?"

Equally mystified, Mollie shrugged. "Aunt EJ is all about comfort food. Miss IdaLee prefers baking cakes. And Miss GeorgeAnne's idea of haute cuisine amounts to putting dill relish on top of deviled eggs at the annual church picnic."

Then it came to her.

She sighed. "This has Kara MacKenzie written all over it."

"The Mason Jar owner?"

Mollie nodded. "Kara's also a world-class chef. The matchmakers farmed out our Valentine's fondue night."

"You mean our *fun*-due night."

A corner of his mouth quirked, and the bottom dropped out of her stomach. Why did her pretend husband have to be so stinking handsome and charming?

She steadied her breath. "Thank you for being a good sport."

Colton offered her his arm. She slipped her hand in the crook of his elbow. Perhaps the evening wouldn't be as terrible as she feared.

He winked. "Let the fun-due begin."

Indeed.

Chapter Six

Colton surveyed the feast the matchmakers had laid out for them.

Two plates. Two fondue forks. Chocolate and cheese fondue pots.

"Looks like they went all out." He stood by Mollie's side. "The Double Name Club thought of everything."

She rolled her eyes. "'Cause nothing shrieks romance like fondue, right?"

They grinned at each other. The awkwardness between them fled.

"Would you scooch the table closer to the couch?" She gestured. "We can pull the pillows around and lean against the side of the sofa. After standing on my feet all day, I'm not getting any younger."

He raised his eyebrows. "You are plenty young. And beautiful, too."

"Thank you," she stammered.

He shouldn't have said that, but it was true. She looked amazing. The last time he'd seen her so dressed up was at the courthouse. The day they got married. He rubbed the back of his neck.

Dropping his gaze, he maneuvered the coffee table into position for her, careful not to upset the items on top. She settled on one of the cushions and patted the pillow beside her.

He tucked his legs under the coffee table and plucked a white paper from between fluted glasses. "Our instructions."

She raised an eyebrow. "We need instructions to eat fondue?"

He smiled. "Apparently, we do."

"What does it say?"

He skimmed the page. "While we eat, we're supposed to answer questions. The cheese is first. Then the chocolate. And there's one rule—whoever drops something into the pot has to kiss their date."

Leaning over his arm, she read the paper for herself. "We're also supposed to record the evening." She picked up a small instant camera, nestled next to the vase of tulips.

He glanced at her over the top of the paper. "To add to our wedding album."

"We don't have a wedding album," she pointed out.

"But we'll have fun-due night covered."

Smiling, she inched closer. "How about a selfie to kick things off?"

Colton grinned. "Great idea." Holding his arm out, their heads together, he snapped a picture. A citrusy tang wafted off her skin. She smelled as good as she looked.

He set aside the camera. "No more photos until we eat."

"Agreed."

For the next few moments, they munched happily.

She looked over the instruction sheet. "First question. 'Who do you respect the most and why?'"

He reached for an apple slice. "You—for the sacrifices you've made for your mom, Olly and me."

Mollie waved away his words. "It isn't a sacrifice to be there for the people you—" She bit her lip. "People you care about."

Something unfamiliar stirred in his heart. He knew she loved him as a friend. What would it be like to be truly loved by her? In a relationship that went beyond friendship.

Those she loved, she loved deeply and well. No one had ever loved him like that, not even Erin. The man who won Mollie's heart would be blessed beyond measure.

Colton found himself longing for something he'd not understood he wanted. But insubstantial as dandelion fluff, borne aloft on winds of fear, the fulfillment of his heart's desire floated out of reach.

To cover his confusion, he speared a meatball and dipped it into the cheese pot. Pretend marriage or not, Mollie would never think of him as anything other than a friend.

"What about you?" he mumbled. "Who do you

respect the most?" He stuffed the meatball into his mouth.

"My mom. I would never have been so brave and strong."

He frowned. "You're brave and strong in the everyday choices you've made. To return to Truelove. To care for Oliver. To run your mom's salon. To be there for your dad."

"To marry you…" She threw him a teasing smile. "What was I thinking?"

"Not one of your better decisions."

She nudged him with her shoulder. "So far, so good." She smiled. "As long as there's chocolate, right?"

"I was kidding the other day." He looked at her. "Besides my son, you are absolutely my favorite person in the whole world."

She batted her lashes at him. "Why thank you, kind sir. I can't think of anyone I'd rather be fake married to than you."

They laughed.

He'd missed her. He'd missed this. The way they were with each other.

"Okay…" Her mouth curved. "Next question. 'In what ways are you the same and different?'" She jabbed him with her elbow. "Be nice."

"We both love Olly."

She nodded.

"We both like fish tacos."

She smoothed out her dress. "I think the proper word is 'adore.'"

"We're both—" his eyes scoured the ceiling, searching for inspiration "—really, really good at karaoke."

She rolled her eyes. "Differences?"

"You like people and I don't."

She pursed her lips. "That's because I'm an extrovert."

"And I'm antisocial." His mouth quirked. "Isn't that what you called me the other day?"

She wagged her fork at him. "Was I wrong?"

"Nope." He grinned. "Although, between coming home to you and acting as a project manager, I'm using more words on a daily basis than usual."

She shot him a funny look, and he realized what he'd let slip about *coming home*. To her. Flames licked at his neck. Sweat peppered his forehead.

"You've been such a help to Dad. He says you're a natural leader, keeping everyone on schedule."

Eager to take the conversation in another direction, he reached across her to snag a slice of salami. "This week I discovered I not only enjoy working with your dad, but I like the work, too."

Mollie stuck her fork into a potato. "What do you enjoy about it?"

"Seeing the houses come together is interesting. Knowing we're putting together a good product in which families will make memories is gratifying." He ducked his head and dragged a carrot stick through the cheese. "At the end of the day, it makes me feel like I've accomplished something worthwhile. Not only me, though. Every member of the crew has an important job. The Army taught me to appreciate working with a team."

"Wow. So many words." She threw him an exaggerated, wide-eyed look. "Hope you didn't use up your quota already."

"Hush, you." He bumped shoulders with her. "It would serve you right if I went zero dark silent on you the rest of the evening."

"I'm teasing. I'm happy you love what you do. Maybe you've found your calling."

Perhaps so, but not a vocation he intended to practice long-term in Truelove. Yet there was no point in rubbing it in her face and ruining the evening.

He picked up the white sheet. "'Something you're glad you'll never have to do again.'" He squared his shoulders. "Like marry me."

She stiffened. "Is that how you feel?"

"No..." Frowning, he searched her face. "So far, so good." He placed his hand next to hers on the cushion. Their pinkies touched. "And as long as there's chocolate, right?"

Something eased in her eyes.

Mollie lifted her chin. "In regards to the question, I don't want to take someone I love to chemo ever again." Her mouth trembled. "Or fear uniformed men with bad news are going to knock on my door."

"I don't ever want to go to war again. Or bury the mother of my child."

Their gazes locked.

Pinpricks of mutual awareness danced down his spine.

Breaking eye contact, she took the paper from him. "What's the next question?" She read for a second. "Oh."

"What is it?"

A soft smile flitted at the corners of her lips. "'Favorite memory of us.'"

"That's easy."

She helped herself to a pretzel. "You go first then."

"Favorite memory of us is my first day at Truelove Elementary. Fifth grade. On the playground. I was sitting on a bench. All alone."

She shook her head. "You were sitting alone because you were rude to the kids who tried to include you in their games."

He threw her a playful glance. "Didn't stop you from walking straight up to me to tell me we were going to be best friends."

She smirked. "I was right, wasn't I?"

"About most things, but don't let it go to your head."

That day in fifth grade, he'd just been moved to his ninth foster home in as many years. He'd been scared and trying not to show it. He was sick of always being the new kid in school.

Sometimes bullied. Often made fun of. The worst, however, was when he was pitied. He was the weird kid whose parents hadn't loved him enough to keep him.

Recess and lunch were the hardest. When it became awkwardly obvious he didn't fit in. It was difficult to make new friends, and within a week, a month, a year he might be forced to pull up stakes, move again and have to say goodbye. By the second grade, he'd learned it was easier not to form any attachments at all.

Until the bubbly little girl, whose grandmother lived two doors down from his current foster family, walked across the playground and made her pronouncement.

Mollie popped a cherry tomato in her mouth, chewed and swallowed. "You said you didn't want to be my friend."

"Which didn't deter you in the slightest. You plopped yourself beside me and proceeded to give me a briefing on the town and the gentlefolk of Truelove."

She winked. "You're welcome."

"Me getting up and walking away didn't help." He tweaked her nose with the tip of his finger. "Persistent and annoying as a mosquito. You still are."

"Never could take a hint."

He shook his head. "With you dogging my every step, we must have made a dozen turns around the playground before recess ended."

"But we sat together at lunch and talked."

"You talked." He rolled his eyes. "A steady stream of chatter."

She made a show of fluffing her hair. "An essential skill for a future hairdresser."

He'd never before met anyone like her. Nor since. "By lunchtime, I decided you weren't a normal person."

She laughed. "And now?"

"Jury's still out."

With mock outrage, she poked his ribs. Chuckling, he fell over onto the pillows.

That long-ago day had been the real beginning of his life. After school, she walked him back to his new housing situation. She'd badgered him into meeting her grandmother—whose cookies proved an easy bribe. Eventually, he met Mollie's parents. The rest was history—his history.

All because a little girl with auburn tints in her hair and a sparkle in her eyes decided to be his friend.

He swirled a cube of bread through the cheese. "Molls."

She crunched on an apple slice. "Yeah?"

Keeping his head down, he concentrated on doing a thorough job of coating the bread with cheese. "There's one question about that day I always wanted to ask you."

She waved her fork at him. "Ask away."

"Why me?" He looked at her. "Why did you choose me to be your best friend?"

Mollie got lost in the blue liquid of his gaze.

She could hardly believe the first time they met was his favorite memory. Something as warm as melted cheese pooled in her belly.

"Mollie..." He snagged hold of her wrist. "Don't dodge the question. Why did you want to be best friends with me?"

Why *had* she marched over to him? It was hard to think with his hand on her arm. His touch sent her nerve endings tingling.

"Please tell me, Mollie. I really want to know."

The answer came to her with stark, crystal clarity.

"Because you looked like you needed choosing," she whispered.

"Thank you," he rasped.

He circled her wrist with his thumb and forefinger. A tiny gesture but it contained the entire world.

"Without you and your family, I shudder to think where I would be now. Dead or in jail most likely. There would definitely not have been an Olly."

"There should never be a world where there is no Olly."

"Agreed." Flashing her a quick smile, he grabbed a handful of tomatoes. "So what's your favorite memory of us?"

"There are too many to choose only one."

"Don't make me report you to the Double Name Club for failure to cooperate, Molls."

"Oh, I don't know..." She scrounged for the last meatball. "But if you're going to make me choose... maybe the time when you tried to teach me how to drive a stick shift."

He snorted. "A skill you've yet to master."

"Or the time we boycotted the prom and went to the Burger Barn instead."

He smiled. "We should take Oliver there."

"I can't decide on a favorite memory." She opened her hands. "Maybe because my favorite memory of us is a memory that's yet to happen."

He pointed his fork at her. "That right there is the biggest difference between us."

"What?"

"You and your rose-colored, glass half-full, silver lining, the-sun-will-shine-tomorrow kind of thinking."

She gave him a look. "As opposed to glass half-empty, cloud-on-the-horizon, no-hope-in-sight sort of thinking?"

"Exactly."

She pursed her lips. "I think it takes more courage to keep the faith."

"As the recipient of so much of your faith in me, who am I to argue with that?"

They shared a small smile.

"Enough of the serious talk. What's the next instruction?"

He scanned the paper. "'Feed your sweetheart a chocolate-dipped strawberry.'"

She sat forward. "I've been dying to dive into the chocolate."

Holding a berry by its green cap, she swirled the end in the creamy milk chocolate. "Open up the tunnel, soldier. Here comes the strawberry."

"You've been spending way too much time with a toddler."

"Stop moving." She aimed for his mouth. "Oops." She grinned at the smudge of chocolate on his cheek. "Missed."

He swiped at his face. "You did that on purpose."

"I did not. You're too wiggly."

"How about we see how you like some chocolate face paint of your own." He made a sudden move.

Squealing in feigned terror, she scooted out of his reach. "Too quick for you, Atkinson." She grabbed the list off the coffee table. "Next… 'Throw a grape in the air and see if your sweetheart can catch it in their mouth.'"

"I'm game."

She tossed him one seedless grape at a time. He made heroic and hilarious attempts to catch them. She snapped a few photos of his efforts. They laughed so hard they collapsed against the sofa.

Mollie blew out a breath. "Who knew the Double Name Club could throw such a great fondue party?"

He stretched his legs under the coffee table. "This has been fun."

"Because it's fun-due."

He made a groaning sound. "Same silly Mollie Drake you were at ten."

"Don't forget it's Mollie Atkinson now." She made a sweeping gesture toward the coffee table. "Hence, the belated Valentine occasion."

An artery pulsed in his jaw. "I haven't forgotten."

When he looked at her, she found it hard to breathe.

Slightly discombobulated, she grabbed her fork. She stabbed at a chunk of bread, but it fell off the fork and disappeared beneath the cheese.

Her heart thudded. "Oh." She looked at the pot then raised her gaze to Colton.

Colton's eyes glinted with mischief. "You've done it now."

Experiencing a sliver of panic, she touched her finger to her mouth. "It was an accident."

"You know the rule." He leaned forward. "Time to pay up, Molls."

Feeling herself on the precipice of the unknown, she blinked rapidly. "Kiss you, you mean?"

She gulped. Over the years, more than a tiny part of her had pondered what it would be like to kiss Colton. Wondered… Hoped… Dreamed…

His hand dropped to her waist, pulling her closer. Her gaze jerked to his. She held back, trying to get a read from his features. Did he want her to kiss him?

In that agonizing eternity of a split second, something shifted in his eyes. Her breath hitched.

His face lifted. "Mollie…"

She tilted her head. Closing her eyes, she brushed her mouth against his.

He tasted like she'd imagined, only better. With a yummy dash of chocolate thrown in for good measure. Infinitely sweet. Gentle. Totally beguiling. Her heart sped up.

She pulled back a fraction. They stared at one another. Close enough their breath comingled. Their lips not quite touching.

His eyes went heavy-lidded. And just like that, the atmosphere between them heightened. Their silly play-by-the-rule kiss became charged with something of far more substance.

Colton slipped his hand around the nape of her neck. He tugged her closer.

Her lips parted in anticipation. His mouth came down on hers. Her insides somersaulted. Colton finally was going to—

The doorbell rang.

Jolting, they sprang apart.

Chest heaving, Colton swallowed hard. His Adam's apple bobbed in his throat. Her eyes wide, she looked about how he felt.

Gobsmacked.

The first, playful kiss had been one thing... The second kiss, although seemingly spontaneous, hadn't been as random as he'd like to believe. What he'd felt after her lips brushed his—the depth of emotion had taken him by surprise.

And his intent to return the kiss, albeit cut short, hadn't come out of nowhere.

She put a shaky hand to her throat. As shaky as he felt right now. Over the years, he'd thought about what it would be like to kiss Mollie. He rubbed his mouth. He wondered no more.

If that was even a small indication of what a

true, proper kiss with Mollie would be like… Wow. Just wow.

The doorbell rang again. Sharp. Insistent. He scrambled to his feet and nearly upset the coffee table in his haste.

She gave him a curious look, but she didn't comment on what happened between them. What *almost* happened between them.

What had almost happened? His heart thundered. Nothing. But this would not do.

He stared at her. Her breath came in short, little spurts. This would not do at all.

For a host of reasons, he and Mollie were a bad idea. Best friends forever. Pretend husband and wife only for the time being.

But once Oliver was comfortable with him… Once Mollie's mom was better… Once spring ended… Their pretending must end, too.

What had he been thinking?

Yet the moment her mouth grazed his, he'd stopped thinking and just reacted. Responding to a deep-seated yearning he hadn't realized was there.

The doorbell rang a third time.

Mollie held out her hand to him. "We need to answer that."

"Saved by the bell."

He pulled her to her feet. But the touch of her skin against his ignited tingles of electricity that raced up his arm.

Colton dropped her hand like it was a grenade.

And took a giant step back. “Leastways, we finally got that out of our systems.”

Sparks of anger glinted in her eyes. “Is that what we did?”

Jamming his hands in his pockets, he feigned a nonchalance he was far from feeling. “Probably inevitable. Been there. Done that. Box ticked. Case closed.”

Her mouth tightened.

At a sudden, determined hammering on the door, she spun on her heel. Giving him a nice, cold view of her shoulder, she threw open the door.

“Mowee!” Oliver cried, straining for her.

She caught his son in her arms.

Amber threw Colton a sheepish smile. “The longer the night wore on, the more we were unable to console him. He wanted his teddy. He wanted his bed. Most of all, he wanted his Mollie.”

Mollie hugged his son. “Hey, sweetie pie. No need to cry. I’m here.”

He buried his face in her neck. “Me want Mowee.” He hiccuped in the way children did after a long bout of tears.

Patting his back, she nodded. “We aren’t used to being apart at night.”

Amber handed Colton the black backpack. “Sorry to cut your evening short.”

“It’s fine.” She darted a look at him. “We were done here.”

The inflection in her voice struck him as ominous.

But good thing Amber came when she did. Who

knew what lengths of emotional folly the second kiss might have led to?

Like maybe even a third?

So why even now did his lips still thrill at the memory of her mouth against his? His fingertips continued to burn with the remembered feel of the smooth skin on the nape of her neck. He rubbed his hand against his side.

Good thing nothing happened. Yeah. Right.

It was for this reason—the pitfall of romantic entanglement—that the pact between them existed. He was determined to do everything in his power to ensure this never happened again. Yet the idea of never again kissing Mollie brought him no comfort. Only a strange, aching disappointment.

As for his new resolve?

He had an inkling it might be easier made than kept.

Chapter Seven

On Monday morning after her client departed, Mollie swept the area around the chair. She had the salon to herself.

She hadn't slept well over the weekend. She and Colton had been subdued with each other. It felt like there'd been a perceptible shift between them. He made himself noticeably absent from the house when the matchmakers arrived the next morning to help her clean up from the fondue night.

Mollie caught the three women exchanging anxious looks, but she was thankful none of them asked any questions. Aunt EJ had always been perceptive. Mollie's face probably told the story. Nothing else needed to be said.

She was tired on more than a physical level. And confused.

His kiss had felt far more meaningful than the first playful kiss that prompted it. It had been Colton who initiated the second kiss, hadn't it?

Massaging her forehead, she leaned against the broom. She hadn't imagined what happened between them. Although, it was clear from his reaction, the kiss hadn't meant the same thing to him as it had to her.

Now she felt stupid. And delusional. And humiliated. He must think she was so pathetic. And needy. And possibly even repulsive.

Her cheeks burned. With unaccustomed vigor, she swept the remains of the haircut into the dustpan and tossed it into the bin.

No matter her feelings to the contrary, he wasn't attracted to her. No amount of wishful thinking would change that. She needed to accept reality and stop dreaming of a life she couldn't have with him and Olly.

Setting aside the broom, she scrubbed at her eyes. Reality stabbed like a pair of scissors into her heart. She wanted nothing so much as to run to her mom and pour out her hurt. But of course, she couldn't.

Mollie couldn't talk to anyone about her mess of a marriage. She almost wished she'd never crossed the playground that long-ago day. Never met Colton Atkinson. Never fallen in—

She couldn't contain the sob that burst from her throat. She covered her mouth with her hand. Tears rolled unchecked down her cheeks.

The bell above the door jangled.

"What's wrong?" Shayla's voice sharpened. "What's happened?" In two strides, her friend crossed the salon. "Is it your mom?"

Mollie shook her head.

"Is this about Olly?"

Mollie swiped at her eyes. "Olly is great."

"Colton?"

Eyes brimming, she turned away.

"I can't imagine how difficult it must be to try to reconnect with your husband after months of separation. You must feel like strangers."

Gripping the salon chair, Mollie squeezed her eyes shut. "It's not what you think. It's an impossible situation, and I am such a fool."

Shayla touched her arm. "You are not a fool."

Forlorn, Mollie gazed at their reflections in the mirror.

Shayla squeezed her shoulder. "You know the difficult path I walked to get to where Luke and I are now. The secrets I kept to protect myself from Jeremiah's abusive biological father."

"You and Jeremiah were in physical danger. My secrets are about trying to save face." Mollie sagged against the chair. "I'm embarrassed and heartsick. There's my mom's health to consider. And Olly's future."

Shayla turned her away from the mirror. "I'm here for you, Mollie. That's what friends are for. To listen. To stand by us when hope seems lost."

Mollie chewed the inside of her cheek.

"If you ever need to talk to someone, there'd be no judgment from me."

Mollie's mouth quivered. "I've ruined everything with Colton."

Shayla's eyebrows rose. "According to the grapevine, fondue night was a great success. Very romantic."

Mollie burst into tears. "Too romantic." The need to unburden herself became overwhelming. She was drowning in the secrets. "The marriage isn't real. None of it. It's all a lie," she sobbed.

Shayla's eyes widened. "You and Colton aren't married?"

Mollie wrapped her arms around herself. "We're married, but not for the reason everyone believes."

Shayla led her over to the empty reception area. "I don't understand." She pulled Mollie onto the settee.

Burying her face in her hands, Mollie told Shayla how a widowed Colton had found himself about to be deployed with no one to take care of his son. How her mom's illness necessitated her decision to relocate to Truelove. And then, Colton's surprising proposal.

"Why did you marry him?" Shayla held up her hand. "Don't use Oliver as your excuse. I know how deeply you care for Olly, but I'm not buying that as your real motivation for marrying his father."

"You're right." She took a shuddery breath. "I married Colton because I've loved him since we were teenagers. Without hope of anything ever happening between us. When Colton proposed out of the blue..." Tears welled anew.

Shayla gave her a moment to regain her composure.

Mollie fretted the frayed rip at the knee of her

jeans. "It felt like my chance with him had finally come. I wanted to marry him so badly. For so long. So I said yes. I was sure he would grow to love me."

When Shayla said nothing, Mollie rushed to fill the void. "I know now how foolish that was, because he won't allow himself to love me other than as a friend. That's all he wants from me. All he ever has or ever will want from me."

"Your parents don't know?"

Mute with misery, Mollie shook her head.

"I never had the kind of relationship with my parents you have with yours. Trust is a fragile, precious thing. The truth has a way of coming out at the worst possible time. My secret almost cost me Luke."

Mollie's friend looked out the window over the square. "You need to tell your parents what's going on. They love you. They'll understand. Better they hear it from you than from someone else."

"I know," she whispered.

"You also need to tell him how you feel."

Mollie shook her head. "We promised not to fall in love with each other." She explained about their ill-fated teenage friendship pact.

Shayla stared at her. "Anyone with eyes in their head could see how it was between you two, even in high school."

"He doesn't love me." Mollie leaned against the chair. "We're only keeping up the pretense until Mom gets the results from her scan. And until Olly is more comfortable with his dad."

"Then what did you mean about fondue night being too romantic?"

In for a penny… Mollie gave her a thumbnail version of their first kiss and Colton kissing her back.

"That kiss doesn't sound like nothing to me. Or remotely in compliance with your friendship-only pact."

"It was a mistake that will never happen again." Mollie laced her hands together. "Colton's clear about not wanting anything beyond friendship."

"So clear he proposed to you?" Shayla cocked her head. "Something isn't adding up. If him kissing you back last night indicates anything, he feels more for you than you think. And he's confused."

"He isn't the only one," she muttered. "But he's lost everyone he ever allowed himself to love. He won't let anyone into his heart, except Olly. There can never be a future for us."

"I'm sorry." Shayla unlocked Mollie's hands and held them in hers. "I'm here for you whenever you need to talk to someone. I'll be praying for you both."

Shayla was a dear friend.

"Thank you."

"Don't wait too long to talk to your parents." She put her arm around Mollie. "I'm not saying it won't be hard, but they need to hear the truth from you first."

The singer glanced at the clock and rose. "Gotta pick up Jeremiah. But I almost forgot… Thought you might appreciate a heads-up." Shayla slipped the strap of her purse on her shoulder. "The Double Name Club was having a planning meeting at the Jar while I was at breakfast with Luke's mom."

Mollie groaned. "Please tell me the agenda didn't involve another date night for Colton and me."

"Don't shoot the messenger, but forewarned is forearmed."

Mollie blew out a breath. "Go ahead. Let me have it. What are the matchmakers planning for us this week?"

"A spa night and a couples massage were mentioned."

"Just when I think the situation can't get any more embarrassing..."

Shayla gave her a commiserating smile. "Welcome to Truelove." She fluttered her fingers at Mollie and headed out.

Propping her elbows on her knees, Mollie cradled her head in her hands.

When she and Olly first returned to Truelove, it seemed easier to let everyone believe something that wasn't true. But Shayla was right. The truth was bound to come out.

The longer she delayed, the worst the final revelation. The dominos were starting to fall. One after the other. Things had gotten complicated, thanks to the matchmakers. She and Colton were losing control of the situation.

He would have a fit when she told him this latest development. And rightly so. She wouldn't blame him if he ditched this sham marriage, took his son and ran for his life.

* * *

Colton met Ethan for lunch at the Mason Jar.

Mollie's grandma and Ethan's grandma, Erma-Jean, had been sisters. Their grandchildren—Ethan and Mollie—shared similar traits of warm open-heartedness.

In addition to relaying his children's latest antics, Ethan told Colton about the father who'd abandoned him and his mother. Surprising himself, Colton related his own troubled childhood and his concerns about the failure to bond with Oliver.

Like his cousin, Ethan was a good listener. He encouraged Colton not to give up hope. They talked about getting together for lunch again soon. Colton looked forward to it. Ethan was a good guy.

After he left to return to his own work, Colton remained in the booth and rolled out the blueprints of the housing development. The neighborhood he was helping his father-in-law build was located between Truelove and Asheville.

His not-for-real father-in-law. He raked his hand over his head. The lines of reality were beginning to blur.

Studying the house plans, he became aware of a strident voice from the table underneath the bulletin board. The matchmaker table.

He glanced up. GeorgeAnne was holding forth with her Double Name Club cronies. And as usual, not bothering to lower her voice. Probably planning a corporate coup. Or, he smirked, world domination.

Colton returned to his perusal of the design. But like an annoying mosquito, GeorgeAnne droned on. Making notes on his phone, he tuned her out.

Until "Mollie" and "date night" pierced through to his consciousness.

Pretending to examine the drawings, he unashamedly eavesdropped. The best defense often required a strong offense. If the opportunity presented itself, there was nothing wrong with intelligence-gathering.

It wasn't like he could help overhearing their conversation. Everybody on the other side of the mountain could probably hear her, too.

"…worn out from worrying about her mom…" GeorgeAnne said.

"On her feet all day, running the salon," ErmaJean added.

He fidgeted.

"Taking care of a toddler, too," IdaLee interjected.

His son could be a handful.

"She's exhausted. Utterly exhausted." GeorgeAnne warmed to her theme. "Which is why Mollie deserves a spa night with her new husband."

He blinked.

"A mani-pedi," GeorgeAnne's sister, CoraFaye Dolan, added.

His gaze flicked in the direction of the matchmakers.

"Write that down," ErmaJean directed Martha Alice Breckenridge. "A facial, too."

GeorgeAnne lifted her bony index finger. "Don't forget the crowning event of the evening—the couples massage."

Whoa.

Not that Mollie didn't deserve pampering. But a couples massage? He blushed to the roots of his hair.

"A couples massage…" IdaLee went starry-eyed. "I remember when Charles and I—"

"Nobody wants to hear about your marital massages, IdaLee," GeorgeAnne growled.

"So romantic." ErmaJean beamed.

"So dreamy." CoraFaye clasped her hand over her heart.

So not happening.

Grabbing hold of the edge of the table, he swung out of the booth. This was outrageous. Mollie would be mortified.

He stalked toward the matriarchs of matchmaking. "Ladies…" He clenched his teeth.

"Oh, my." Martha Alice's eyelashes fluttered. "I guess you overheard our little surprise."

He prayed for self-restraint. Prayer—something he'd done a lot more of lately. Truelove often had that effect on people.

Colton opened his hands in a conciliatory gesture. "While Mollie and I appreciate your efforts to make these date nights so…so…" He paused, at a loss.

IdaLee patted his arm. "Special?"

CoraFaye raised her eyebrow. "Memorable?"

He tried again. "I'm glad I ran into y'all. I've had some thoughts of my own about our date nights."

ErmaJean grinned. "Do tell."

Her expression unreadable, GeorgeAnne said nothing.

A fairly ominous sign, but taking hold of his courage, he plunged ahead. "I was thinking it would mean more to Mollie if I took over the planning."

"How delightful and altogether proper," IdaLee gushed.

"What are your thoughts?" GeorgeAnne barked.

"Um…uh…" Spur of the moment, he had no thoughts. He groped for something to say. "Like… taking Mollie to revisit places we used to go when we were teenagers."

IdaLee nodded. "When you were secretly in love."

"But wouldn't admit it to yourself, much less each other," ErmaJean enthused.

Okay… Kind of specific. And thought-provoking on a whole different level.

"Something like that," he rasped.

His gaze cut from one end of the group to the other. Finally, his eyes landed on GeorgeAnne. "What do you think?"

"It has potential." Her thin lips thinned even further. "But I reserve the right to consult on your upcoming anniversary celebration. Agreed?" She extended her hand.

He shook her hand. She squeezed his hand hard. He resisted the urge to wince.

"Don't let us down, Atkinson." She gave him the stink eye. "Nor that sweet bride of yours, either."

"No, ma'am." He eased his battered paw from her grip. "Absolutely not. Wouldn't dream of it." He beat a hasty retreat, snatched up the blueprints and exited the café.

On the sidewalk, feeling as if he'd dodged a bullet, he started toward his truck. But he had a sudden thought.

The Truelove grapevine would make quick work of ensuring Mollie learned about the proposed spa night. No need to give her one more thing to worry about. Not on his watch. Not while he could lighten her burdens.

Feeling protective, he strode toward the hair salon. A few blocks from the café, he stood underneath the black-and-white-striped awning. He yanked open the door to a flurry of bells.

A chemical smell immediately assaulted his nostrils. Followed by a scent with more pleasant, flowery undertones from the hair products she used in the salon.

Coming in from the bright sunshine, he let his eyes adjust. Not much had changed since Glenda ran the salon. Mollie's mom loved pink, and the salon reflected her tastes. The wallpaper was a striped pink and white. The effect was utterly elegant and totally feminine.

He'd never been one to venture into Hair Raisers, except on pain of death when Mollie had forced him to accompany her. Usually on an errand to extort milkshake money from her fun-loving mom. He felt as out of place now as he had then.

In the reception area, a gaggle of chattering women, magazines in hand, went silent. In various stages of color treatments, the women wore bright pink capes over their clothes.

Standing at the salon chair by the mirror, Mollie had gone stock-still. The hair spray can in her hand hovered over the head of their neighbor, Mrs. Desmond. Seated at their feet on the black-and-white-checked floor, a small Chihuahua yipped a welcome to him.

He took a good look at Mollie. She appeared much the same since he'd seen her at breakfast. But at some point, she'd gathered her hair off her neck and secured it with a clip into a messy bun on the top of her head. Something about the upswept hair, her effortless glamour, grabbed hold of him. And he really looked at her.

At the blue jeans with the fashionable hole at the kneecap. The sturdy but stylish wedges on her feet. She wore a long-sleeved tee that made her eyes more gray than blue.

Light from the window overlooking the square highlighted the cute sprinkle of freckles on her nose. He was struck—surely not for the first time?—by her girl-next-door prettiness.

"Colton?"

He jerked. How long had she'd been trying to get his attention?

"Is something wrong?"

He scratched his head. “Would it be possible for us to have a private word?”

“Privacy is overrated,” one of the women spouted. The other ladies laughed.

He stuffed his hands into his jean pockets. “Only in Truelove.”

Which caused them to hoot harder.

“Just one minute, Mrs. Desmond.” Mollie flashed him a sympathetic look. “I’ll be right back.”

“I’ll finish her for you.” One of GeorgeAnne’s daughters-in-law jumped up from her chair in the reception area. “I can spray hair as well as the next person.”

Mollie handed her the can and led him to a secluded corner in the hallway near a closet-sized room her mom always referred to as her office.

“I ran into the matchmakers at lunch,” he whispered. No doubt, the waiting room strained to hear their every word. “Your aunt EJ and the rest of her cohort were having a planning meeting.”

“That’s weird.” She tapped her chin. “I heard they had a meeting over breakfast. Two meetings in one day seems strange, even for them.”

“I wanted to let you know about our next date night.”

She let her head fall against the wall. “I apologize in advance for their machinations. They think they’re helping us.”

He wasn’t as sure about that as Mollie seemed to be. But she always gave everyone the benefit of the doubt, including him. When they'd long since ceased to deserve it. Including him.

"So you know about spa night?" Saying the words made his nose crinkle.

"I can't tell you how sorry I am." She closed her eyes. "This is over-the-top, even for them. I dare not contemplate how they plan to pull this off."

"No worries. It's not happening. I had a talk with GeorgeAnne."

Mollie's eyes flew open. "You what?"

"I took care of it."

A look of horror befell her features. "There is no fixing it when those women get an idea in their heads."

"I told them I was taking over the planning of our date nights."

Her eyes went wide. "And GeorgeAnne let you live to tell me?"

Colton chuckled. "Actually, in hindsight it wasn't too hard of a sell. She appeared to like my idea."

"Which was?"

Colton braced one hand along the wall beside her head. "Mollie. Mollie. Mollie. Where would be the surprise if I told you now?"

Her lips quirked. "That good, huh?"

Colton's attention fell to her mouth. Something painful sliced through his gut. "It will be as long as you're willing to go out with me Saturday night."

She leaned against the wall, her hands resting in the small of her back. "Colton Atkinson, are you asking me out on a date?"

He smiled. "I guess I am. Saturday okay with you?"

"I think..."

He swallowed, hard. "Yes?"

She smiled. "As your bride, I think something could be arranged." Rising on the tip of her toes, she gave him a swift peck on his cheek. "I look forward to it."

He touched a hand to his face, feeling the imprint of her lips. "Me, too. Molls?"

She fiddled with the gold loop in her earlobe. "Yes?"

"I..." His voice went husky.

A fit of coughing broke the moment. A pungent aroma wafted from the salon.

"Mollie!" Mrs. Desmond coughed. "We need you. She's asphyxiating us in here."

They sprang apart.

Mollie made a face. "Duty calls."

He grinned. "Making the world a more beautiful place, one Truelove hairstyle at a time."

She giggled. He hadn't heard her do that since they were kids. It had the curious effect of making him feel twelve feet tall.

"I need to get to work, too." Yet neither of them moved. "Your father is probably wondering where I am."

"Mollie!" several women hollered.

She unglued herself from the wall. "See you tonight."

"Can't wait."

He floated out behind her into the reception area.

"Newlyweds..." CPA Myra Penry, Lila Gibson's mother, cooed.

"So sweet..." Mayor Watkin's wife batted her eyes.

He decided to ignore the knowing smirks. Yet that afternoon, he found himself whistling snatches of a country song Mollie liked on the radio.

Over the next few days, the cloud of tension between them lifted. As if they'd reached an unspoken truce of sorts.

For Friday night story time with Olly, he selected a book about going on a bear hunt. Flipping through the pages, he scanned the illustrations and previewed the short text. It was based on an old American folk song.

He handed the book to Mollie. "Let's tag-team on this one. You read. Oliver and I can act it out."

"Oooo... Good idea." She sat on the couch. "Olly, this is one of your favorites."

Colton took his place in front of the fireplace. "Let's go on a bear hunt, son."

Oliver climbed onto the sofa next to Mollie.

She and Colton exchanged a look.

Mollie moistened her lips. "Olly, why don't you and Daddy go on a bear hunt together while I read the story?"

He folded his arms. "No."

She blew out an exasperated breath.

Colton broadened his chest. "I'll go on a bear

hunt by myself then." He eyed his son. "The best bear hunt ever."

"No," Olly said.

"Because I'm the best bear hunter." He gritted his teeth. "Ev-er."

Olly sniffed, but said nothing.

"You two are going to be the death of me." She opened the book and began to read. The first obstacle was long grass. "Can't go over it. Can't go under it."

"Gotta go through it." He grabbed an umbrella from the hallstand. Using it like a machete, he pretend-hacked his way through the air.

She snickered. Oliver never cracked a smile.

He threw himself into acting out the moving parts of the story. Encountering a "river," his face superanimated, he did the breaststroke to the other side of the room. Complete with sound effects.

Mollie chuckled. From Olly, he got zilch, zero, nada.

Hamming up the tale of adventure, he squelched his way through icky-sticky mud. Sputtering with laughter, she fell sideways onto a cushion.

At the next bit, he stumbled through the forest. Then shivered through a snowstorm. When he tiptoed into the "cave" with his big, bulky work boots, she laid the book on her lap.

"Stop. Please…" she wheezed. "You're killing me."

At the climax of the story, he grabbed Oliver's teddy bear off the toy chest and wiggled it semi-menacingly. "It's a bear," he cried out in feigned shock.

Olly leaped off the couch. "Me not 'fraid of you, bear!" the little boy shouted.

Colton looked at Mollie. Swallowing a smile, she resumed the story.

Handing the teddy bear to Oliver, Colton reverse-tiptoed-stumbled-squelched-swam-chopped his way "home."

At the end, he threw himself onto the couch beside Mollie. "Whew!" He made a show of wiping his brow. "I'm not going on a bear hunt again."

"Bravo!" She clapped. "You deserve an Academy Award for that performance."

The little boy's lips inched upward.

"That's reward enough." He smiled. "But I wouldn't refuse ice cream. Any in the freezer?"

"Only your favorite, mint chocolate chip." She started to get up.

"You stay put. I'll get it. You've been standing all day." He surged off the couch. "Would you like some ice cream, Olly?"

Clutching the teddy bear, the child stared at him for a second. His brow creased as if his father were a puzzle he was still working out. But solemn as an undertaker, Oliver nodded and followed Colton into the kitchen.

In the freezer, he found two cartons of ice cream—mint chocolate chip and orange sherbet, Mollie's favorite. He removed three small bowls from the cabinet. He did a slow turn, searching for the ice-cream scoop. "Where does she keep the—"

Olly handed him a silver scoop.

His heart melted a little more. "Thank you, son. You're a big help." He dished orange sherbet into a bowl. "Do you want orange sherbet, too?"

"Oliver's favorite is mint chocolate chip like his dad."

They turned at the sound of her voice. Leaning against the doorjamb, she joined them.

Olly nodded. "Chocky mint."

Colton scooped out a smaller portion and handed the bowl and a spoon to his son.

"Thank you." The little boy sat on the mat in front of the sink and dug in.

"You're welcome. Such good manners." He smiled at Mollie.

She smiled back. "It's all in the training. A work in progress." She ambled over to the kitchen island.

He handed Mollie her bowl.

They ate their ice cream and watched Oliver pretend to feed ice cream to his teddy bear.

"He's thawing toward you." Her shoulder rubbed against Colton's. "Like I told you he would. He needed time."

"Note to self—acting silly appeals to his sense of the ridiculous."

"Always worked with his dad." She smirked. "Apples never fall far."

"Ha. Ha. Ha. Very funny." He stuck a spoonful of ice cream into his mouth.

"The truth hurts." Her smile dropped. "I should talk to my parents."

Colton tensed. Everything would change once they went public with the true nature of their not-so-real union. "I just need a little more time, Molls."

"*You* need more time?"

Colton shuffled his feet. "For your mom's sake. Until she gets the results, right?" He cleared his throat. "Besides," he said, motioning to include Olly, "this isn't so bad, is it?"

Her face softened. "No, it isn't." She dipped her spoon into his bowl and took a bite. She rested her head against his bicep. "Not so long as there's chocolate."

Colton crooked his little finger around hers. She let out a gentle sigh. He knew just how she felt.

Truth was, he wasn't ready for any of this to end. From where he stood—from where he'd come from—this house, she and he and Oliver…

It was nothing short of wonderful.

Chapter Eight

The following weeks were a dream come true for Mollie. Full of fun and laughter and "date nights."

Like fish tacos at an upscale restaurant in Asheville. For the sake of nostalgia, milkshakes at the Mason Jar, courtesy of Trudy. And karaoke at a pizza place on the highway.

Not all the dates took place at night. One Saturday, they hiked to a favorite waterfall they'd discovered as teenagers. There were lots of picnics on the wildflower-dotted bluff overlooking the river, near where Amber's dad ran a white water rafting business.

Sometimes Colton arranged for Oliver to have a playdate with Jeremiah or Parker. But mostly, by unspoken mutual agreement, they took the little boy with them. An unorthodox approach to "dating," but when had they ever done anything by the book?

Everything was more fun with the little guy around. It felt like the beginnings of a real family. It was the happiest time she could remember.

On this golden afternoon in late April, they'd stolen away with Olly to feed the ducks in a local pond.

Colton doled out handfuls of cracked corn to Oliver. "The matchmakers still insist on coordinating our so-called first wedding anniversary."

Olly tossed the fistful to the birds in the water.

She let a leaf of lettuce float out to the waiting ducks.

Their "anniversary" fell on the Friday before Father's Day. But a lot could happen in five weeks. She refused to look too far into the future. Or worry about what might never be. She wanted only to enjoy this time with two of her favorite guys in the world.

Oliver chortled at the antics of the ducks. Her eyes met Colton's, and just for a second, held. He smiled.

She smiled back. "As long as our anniversary doesn't involve a couples massage, I think we'll be fine."

"If not a massage, then probably something as equally outrageous." He gave a mock shudder. "But either way, we'll be okay."

For the first time since he returned to Truelove, she believed they just might.

The next week, he called to let her know he was leaving the project site a little early and asked for her and Oliver to be ready to head out for a surprise. She never knew when their next outing would occur. He liked to surprise her. She was amused by his rather boyish urge to keep their dates a secret until he sprung them on her.

Someone called his name. He must have turned away to speak to them. His voice grew muffled, but then he was back with her. "Bring jackets. It could get cool once the sun goes down."

"Will do."

His creativity in putting together the dates amazed her. His commitment to making each one fun warmed her.

Thirty minutes later, when he pulled into the driveway, she and Oliver were waiting for him. Soon, they were on their way. She waved at Mrs. Desmond, who was taking her Chihuahua for an evening stroll.

Leaving the neighborhood, they passed the darkened Mason Jar Café and the bakery, newly opened on Main Street. Most of the downtown businesses were already closed for the day.

The truck clattered over the bridge out of town. Past the recreational center, he took the secondary road that wound over the mountain.

"I've been craving a good ole American meal." He swung into the drive-through of the Burger Barn. "Hamburger, fries, double the pickles, no cheese, right?"

"You remember my usual?"

A favorite burger hangout after football games with their cross-county rival, they hadn't been to the Burger Barn together since high school. When Colton enlisted, she'd moved to the state capital to attend beauty school. After basic training, he moved around the country with the Army. She stayed in Raleigh to work at a salon. Despite the geographical distance, they'd talked weekly and remained best friends.

The truck crept forward in line. He tapped his thumbs on the steering wheel. "A person doesn't forget important things like fast food."

"And for you—a double-stacked, melted cheese, coleslaw with chili on a sesame seed bun."

"You know me well." He nudged his chin at the rearview mirror. "What about the little guy?"

Straining against the straps, Olly pointed at the logo on the building. "Nug, Mowee. Nug."

Colton laughed. "Apparently, Oliver has a usual, too."

Mollie's cheeks went pink. "We don't do fast food often. But Olly loves the chicken nuggets."

"Hey, no criticism meant. You've done an amazing job with him."

The brush of his fingertips against her hand ignited sparks. A tingling sensation traveled to her elbow.

Rolling up to the intercom, he placed their order. After paying and handing the bag to her, he parked next to a group of picnic tables under the dogwood trees. "Too cold to eat outside?"

"It's not too bad. Olly would probably welcome the chance to run off some energy between bites."

When Colton tried to unfasten the buckles on

Oliver's car seat, however, his son became stricken. "Mowee! Mowee!" He held his arms out to her.

Her heart sank. For every step forward, his relationship with Oliver took two steps back.

Jaw clenched tight, Colton moved aside to allow her to take his son. At the table, Oliver scooted close to her, glaring at his father before taking the nugget she held out to him.

Colton sighed. "I can never repay you for what you did for Oliver."

Not this again.

He fiddled with his straw. "When Erin died, you were the only person I wanted to call."

Not meeting his gaze, she gave Oliver a sip from her water cup. Colton hardly mentioned his son's mother. Reinforcing her belief that he must have loved Erin so much he could barely speak of her.

Mollie would have liked to know more about Olly's mother. She wished Colton felt comfortable sharing this brief—but all-important—period of his life. The only period of his life they hadn't shared.

Yet part of her shied away from hearing him declare his love for a woman she'd never met. She'd dated, but no one ever stood a chance with her. There was no room in her heart for anyone but her best friend.

She'd been so excited when he transferred to Fort Liberty. But suddenly, the weekly phone calls stopped. She hadn't understood why.

Until he called to tell her he'd gotten married. And that his wife was expecting a baby. *His wife?*

Quietly devastated for a host of reasons, she'd acquired her first somewhat-serious boyfriend. The next time she heard from Colton was six months later. When he told her about his newborn son, who'd lost his mother.

In the aftermath, Oliver had come to know and love her. The transition from best friend to surrogate mother hadn't felt jarring. Just satisfyingly inevitable.

"Mollie. Hey, Mollie. You okay?"

Jerked out of her reverie, she found Colton's eyes trained on her. Oliver's, too. They'd finished eating. Colton had cleaned up the wrappers, except for the empty french fry carton she clutched like her life depended on it.

"Sorry." Blushing, she rose. "Woolgathering."

He cocked his head. "Penny for your thoughts?"

"These days, thoughts cost more than a penny." She helped Olly slip into his jacket. "Ever hear of a little thing called inflation?"

Chuckling, Colton stuck his hands in his jean pockets. "Mollie. Mollie. Mollie. Do these 'thoughtful' episodes come upon you often?"

"Only when the aroma of fried grease beguiles my Southern heart into a state of bliss." She gave him a gentle bump with her hip. "Was the burger everything you hoped and dreamed?"

His gaze sent a flutter down to her coral-painted toenails. "Beyond all expectation."

Were they were still talking about hamburgers?

Hands stuck in the pockets of his jeans, Oliver wagged his head from one side to the other. "Mowee. Mowee. Mowee."

She glanced at Colton. They burst out laughing.

"Chip off the old block." He grinned. But he was pleased, and she was pleased for him.

"A hard, stubborn knothead of a block." She ruffled the little guy's hair. For good measure, Colton's, too.

"Hey." He ducked out of her reach. "Watch the hair."

Mollie's fingers had itched to touch his hair. She'd no longer been able to ignore the impulse. "Your hair has grown out of its regulation cut."

She tapped her finger against her chin. "Olly could use his first big boy haircut. What do you say we head over to Hair Raisers and trim yours? Maybe your son will want to follow your example."

"Aren't you tired of cutting hair?"

She strapped Oliver into his car seat. "The beautification of an entire community is a sacred duty I take seriously."

He laughed.

At the salon, she sat Olly in the flashy blue hydraulic plastic sportswear chair she'd bought for moms who brought their young children to a hair appointment. It also served as a handy and distracting way to give squirmy kids their own first haircuts.

Watching himself in the mirror, Olly went into pint-size NASCAR mode with much-feigned squealing of brakes and acceleration noises.

Colton sank into the adjacent adult chair. "Remind me never to let him drive a vehicle of mine."

She swirled a cape around his shoulders. He made a face. "Pink? Really?"

Mollie brandished a pair of shears. "It's never smart to insult someone with the ability to end you."

He grinned. "I trust you."

She waggled her eyebrows. "Do you now?"

Colton's mouth quirked. "Mollie..."

Her insides did a nosedive. She had no business looking at his mouth. Reaching for her spray bottle, she spritzed the back of his head with water.

Colton jumped. "That's cold. You could've warned a guy."

"Be still." She combed his hair. "Stop being a baby."

Oliver threw his dad a scornful look. "Me not baby, Mowee."

She smiled. "Daddy's getting a big boy haircut. Do you want me to give you a big boy haircut, Olly?"

Oliver was clearly torn between wanting to be a big boy yet sticking to his anti-Daddy principles. A crease furrowed his brow.

Finally—

"Mowee cut my hair." He bit his lip. "Pwease?"

"The magic word," Colton whispered.

"I'd better cut his hair before he changes his mind." Standing behind Olly, she ran her fingers through his soft brown hair. "I kinda hate to cut off his baby curls."

"Me not baby!" Oliver glowered at her reflection. "Big boy."

Colton folded his arms across his chest. "You heard the man—give him a big boy haircut, Molls."

Blinking away sentimental tears, she got to work. After a few snips, tendrils of baby hair lay scattered on the floor around the chair. "I'm saving one of those curls for his baby book."

"You put together a baby book for him?" He rolled his eyes. "Of course, you did."

"Almost done, sweetie pie. Sit still a few minutes longer."

His blue eyes large and solemn, the little boy stared at himself while she worked.

She shaped Olly's hair to a uniform, shorter length. "There. All finished. Doesn't Oliver look handsome?"

A shy smile curved Olly's mouth as he examined himself in the mirror from every angle. "Me big boy."

Mollie brushed a stray lock of hair off his shirt. "You drive your car while I take care of Daddy's hair, okay?"

Oliver put his hands on the steering wheel. "Big boy haircut wike me."

"Exactly." She ambled over to Colton. "Whew," she rasped. "That went better than I'd hoped."

Colton winked at her. "When you finish with me, will I look as handsome as Oliver?"

"Handsome is as handsome does, Atkinson." She picked up another comb. "Oh, I almost forgot to tell you."

"How already handsome you find me?"

She snorted. "Best get a grip on that big head of yours."

He threw her a teasing grin.

"Olly's class at preschool is having a program next week." She went to work cutting his hair. "Parents are invited. I wasn't sure you could get away from work, but—"

"I'll make the time."

On the day of the program, she arranged to meet him at the preschool, but arrived later than she'd anticipated. Most of the "good" photo-taking seats had already been snagged. Hopefully, they wouldn't have any trouble seeing Oliver, though, once he and his class took the stage.

Giving her a quick smile, Colton slipped into the row of chairs. "I'm not late, am I?"

She moved her handbag so he could take the seat she'd saved for him. "You're just in time." And because it was what she did—or at least that's the excuse she gave herself—she feathered a lock of his hair off his forehead.

Colton ran his hand over his head. "That bad, huh?"

Hardly. With an effort of will, she drew her gaze away from the tanned patch of skin and corded muscles of his neck visible from the open collar of his denim shirt.

Feeling the warmth in her cheeks, she tried playing off her always-visceral reaction to him. "Hairdressers are forever tweaking their creations."

He laughed. "I'm not complaining."

Several moms stopped by to say hello. As usual, her friend Callie McAbee—local photographer and apple orchard owner—had her camera. Her four-year-old son, Micah, would be performing, too.

"How about I get a few pictures of Olly so you and Colton don't have to jockey for position when it's his turn?"

Mollie breathed a sigh of relief. "Thank you."

Callie winked. "Will do." She moved to the front to take her seat.

"What did she mean by jockeying?"

Mollie quirked her eyebrow. "Once this shindig gets going, the aisle and the area below the stage become a madhouse of parents taking videos with their cell phones. Enter at your own risk."

"You're kidding, right? This is a preschool program."

"Awwww, Atkinson..." She smirked. "Your innocence is so cute."

Each group did a brief song. With a sinking heart, she soon realized this was a Mother's Day program.

She dared not glance at Colton. It must kill him not having Oliver's mother here to celebrate with him. Breaking his heart all over again at everything Erin was missing in her son's life.

Olly's class was the last to perform. She'd taken

care to dress the little boy in one of his better white button-down shirts, which still looked reasonably presentable, though half of his shirttail hung out of his khaki shorts. Catching sight of Mollie in the audience, he gave her a big smile and waved.

The children sang an old Russian folk song she recognized from one of the kid CDs Olly had at home. A touching tribute to the love children everywhere felt for their mothers.

Watching Oliver sing his heart out, she felt her own heart swell with love for this child not of her flesh. At the same time, she ached for the mother he would never know. And for Colton, at this pointed reminder of everything he would never be able to share with the love of his life.

Afterward, the parents were invited to visit their children's classrooms and collect them there. Olly met them at the door with his teacher. Mollie made the introductions.

His teacher thanked Colton for his service, which reduced her handsome hero to a painful shyness. Colton never liked the spotlight.

Oliver gave them a tour. When his son took Colton's hand, she could feel not only his surprise, but Colton's pleasure, too. It was exactly as she'd hoped. Slowly but surely, Olly was coming to see his dad as an essential part of his life.

"Don't forget the surprise in your cubby." The petite young teacher smiled at them. "The children have been working on a gift for their mothers."

Oh, no. Her gut knotted. She shot a quick look

at Colton, who appeared unmoved. But he wasn't one to put his emotions on display.

Bidding them farewell, the teacher moved to talk to another parent.

Clutching a white piece of paper and a long-stemmed pink tulip, Olly hurried back to them. Colton shepherded them into the hallway. With a flourish, Oliver handed the paper to her.

His teacher had drawn a stem, two leaves and the round, yellow center of a flower. Olly's pink thumbprints made up the painted petals.

"It's beautiful, isn't it, Molls?" Colton smiled. "Great job, son."

His little chest broadened. "Read, pwease."

Glimpsing the caption near the top of the page, her smile froze.

"Molls?" Colton took the paper from her limp hand. "I'll read it. 'If mothers were flowers, I would pick you. Happy Mother's Day.'"

Grinning, Olly held the pink tulip out to her. Her stomach plummeted to her toes. She put her hand to her throat.

"Mollie?" Colton's eyes flicked to hers. "He's waiting for you to take the flower."

She was such an imposter. Why hadn't she seen this coming? It was bound to happen. Surrounded by other children at preschool, he'd become aware the other kids had mothers, not Mollies. It was only natural he wanted to fit in with his classmates.

"I can't," she rasped. "I'm not his mother."

The little boy's face fell. "Mommy?" His lower lip quivered.

"It's Mollie, Oliver," she stammered. "You call me Mollie."

His face puckered. "No." He pointed the tulip at her. "You, Mommy."

She wrapped her arms around her body. "I'm Mollie."

"No." He shook his head. "You, *my* mommy." A lone tear made a silent, swift trek down his cheek. "Pwease?"

"What's the matter with you, Mollie?" Colton growled.

She tucked and untucked her hair behind her ear. "I'm sorry I'm not Erin," she whispered.

"You're the only mother he knows." He threw open his hands. "Only a mother would've thought to make him a baby book."

Olly dissolved into tears.

Kneeling beside him, Colton put his hand on his son's shoulder. For once, the child didn't shrug him off.

From the time she first held him in her arms when he was only a week old, she'd never been able to ignore his cries. The tears clawed at her heart. Her eyes welled.

Crouching, she gathered him into her arms. "I'm sorry, sweetie pie. Please forgive me. I love your picture. I love you."

The child buried his face in the hollow of her shoulder. "My mommy?"

Berating her own insecurities, she pressed her lips into his hair. "Yes, sweetie. Mommy's here."

He lifted his head. "Mommy..." The self-doubt in his eyes pierced her to the core. Tears shimmering like dewdrops on his cheeks, he held out the crumpled, worse-for-wear flower to her.

She took it from him gladly. "Thank you, Olly. It's so beautiful. I love pink."

He rubbed his eyes. "Me pick you."

Oliver had picked the pink one for her? Or, he'd picked her? Perhaps he meant both.

Nestling him against her heart, she held him close. For the rest of the afternoon after Colton returned to work, she made a special effort to reassure the little boy of her love for him. The wilting, much-abused tulip held pride of place in a vase on the mantel. The picture went on the fridge.

But Olly refused to drift far from her side. She'd temporarily shattered his confidence in his world. She prayed the slip in his faith in her was temporary.

No matter what the future held, she never wanted Oliver to look at her that way again.

Dinner was subdued. Emotionally exhausted, Olly drooped in his booster seat. Colton sat brooding in his chair. No one had much of an appetite.

She swallowed. "I think it would be best if we forego his bath tonight."

"I'll do the dishes." Colton scraped back his chair. "But after you put him to bed, we need to talk."

Oliver offered no protest as she changed him into his pj's and pulled the covers over him. "Me wuv you, Mommy," the drowsy child whispered.

"I love you, too, my sweet boy."

When she emerged from his bedroom, there was no sign of his father. Glancing through the kitchen window, she caught a glimpse of him in the backyard. In the deepening twilight, he'd rolled his shirtsleeves to his elbows. Hands in his pockets, he stared at something beyond the perimeter of the trees only he could see. In profile, his jaw was tight.

Her anxiety ratcheted. He was angry with her. She was angry at herself for what happened this morning. With a heavy heart, she went outside.

Stars winked in the indigo sky.

Colton reviewed the mistakes that had led him to this moment. There had been many. But leaving his son in Mollie's loving embrace hadn't been one of them.

He pinched the bridge of his nose. He'd spent a lot of time throughout the last month contemplating Reverend Bryant's Easter message. On subsequent Sundays, he'd learned so much about God.

Colton learned a lot about himself, too. Most of it, not so praiseworthy.

He'd spent recent weeks observing men like Ethan, Luke and Sam. He longed to be the kind of father Oliver deserved. He longed to be the kind of man someone like Ted could respect.

Colton yearned for the almost undefinable essence of something—someone—he hadn't realized he needed. Like he needed air and sunshine. The same something he'd glimpsed first in the blue-gray eyes of a little girl on a playground in Truelove.

Everything was such a mess. He was a disaster. After this morning, he no longer could imagine taking his son away from Mollie on a permanent basis. His original plan wasn't an option. Alternate arrangements would have to be worked out. Possibly shared custody.

His shoulders tensed.

Colton sensed—without understanding how he knew—that Mollie had joined him. He turned around.

"I'm sorry for how painful this morning must've been for you." She wrung her hands. "Hearing your son call me mommy. By rights, Erin should've been there. I know how much you loved her."

"Loved her?" He shook his head. "I never wished her dead, but we barely knew each other. I'll always be grateful to her for giving me Olly, but I never loved her."

Mollie's mouth opened and closed. He'd shocked her. "Then why did you marry her?"

"Rising through the ranks, I was a thousand miles from Truelove." He tugged at the back of his neck. "I was lonely and missed my best friend."

She tilted her head. "I don't understand."

"After I called to tell you I was expecting a child, only you—give-everyone-the-benefit-of-the-doubt

Mollie—wouldn't have counted back the months and done the math."

"What do you mean?"

He scrubbed his hand over his face. "I made a mistake one night…and got Erin pregnant."

He closed his eyes against the disillusionment on Mollie's face. "But taking a cue from the most honorable man I know—your father—I wanted to marry her. Then I transferred to Fort Liberty. Erin and I weren't happy. We argued all the time. I don't think we would've stayed together."

He scrubbed at his face. "I'm ashamed to say I never loved her. Other than my son, I'm not sure I'm capable of loving anyone."

"That's not true." She seized his arm. "That's not who you are. That's not how I see you."

If only he could be the man reflected in her eyes, even now after she knew the worst about him.

"Colton, look at me…"

Exactly what he mustn't do. Blood pounded in his ears. He mustn't look at her. Yet ever the magnet, Mollie drew his gaze.

A tear had worked its way onto her cheek. Before he checked himself, he wiped it away with his knuckle.

Her eyes widened. The buzzing in his brain quieted. And suddenly, he gathered her in his arms.

He swept his thumb across the apple of her cheek. Then dropped his gaze to her mouth. His heart slammed against his ribcage. Her eyes closed.

Cradling her face, he sifted his fingers through

her hair. He lowered his head. He gave her the opportunity to pull away if she wished. Yet she didn't.

He told himself this was a bad, bad idea. This would destroy their friendship-only pact. But he kissed her anyway. And she kissed him back.

Without hesitation.

Mollie's arms went around his neck. In that instant, getting Mollie Drake "out of his system" had not a remote chance of succeeding.

Heedless of the consequences, in that split second of time, he didn't care. He'd never felt about Erin—about anyone—the way he felt about Mollie.

But insidious as a serpent, images of his past mistakes filtered into his consciousness. He'd hurt Erin by keeping part of himself out of emotional reach. They'd hurt each other.

He couldn't go through that again. He wouldn't put Mollie through that. Unlike losing Erin, losing Mollie would annihilate him. The friendship-only pact existed for the most valid of reasons. The pact represented the sum total of his fears.

Chest heaving, he pushed her away.

Startled, she blinked at him. Her arms reached for him. "Colton…"

Ruthlessly quelling the treacherous ache of his heart, he took a step backward. He raked his hand through his hair. The citrusy scent of her clung to his fingers.

He fled toward the corner of the house.

"We need to talk," she called after him. "Where are you going?"

He yanked the gate open. “I—I just need time to think.”

Then as darkness unfolded, he left her staring after him.

Chapter Nine

Mollie had been blown away by his revelations regarding Erin. She'd had no idea. She'd assumed... She'd assumed wrong.

Over the next few weeks, she thought about the kiss a lot.

During Martha Alice's weekly shampoo and set. While she trimmed auto repair shop owner Zach's hair—almost a disaster. But with the NASCAR baseball cap he wore twenty-four seven, nobody would notice. Probably...

So yeah. She was struggling to concentrate. But Colton, apparently not so much. She saw little of him.

Despite living in the same house, he managed to avoid spending any time alone with her. No more shared stories about their respective days. Or laughter. Or anything.

He acted like a painfully polite stranger, which made her feel off-kilter. She alternated between wanting to scream, punch his arm or kiss him until he came to his senses. Sometimes all three at the same time.

But a person either loved you or they didn't.

She sensed their time together might be coming to an end. Her mom's results were due early next week after the Memorial Day weekend. She was praying for her mother to be cancer-free. Olly was also feeling more comfortable with his dad.

Oftentimes in the evenings, he "allowed" Colton to sit beside him on the rug in the living room while he played with his toy trucks.

Soon Colton would leave Truelove with his son forever. Leave her forever. The memory of their kiss would have to last her a lifetime.

Mollie hardly could bear to think of a future without them in it. Any future without them would be a bleak one.

That Sunday evening, once again father and son sat on the rug together. Making vroom-vroom noises, Olly raced his toy trucks around the rug.

On the sofa, she flipped through the pages of a magazine. Before the kiss, there would have been banter and laughter between her and Colton, but now only a crackling silence existed.

Picking up on the tension, Oliver fell silent. His eyes darted between them. His forehead puckered.

She ached from the brittle, unspoken strain. They couldn't go on this way. "We need to talk about what happ—"

"That's the last thing we need to do." Colton's mouth flattened. "Words can never be unsaid. Better to say nothing at all."

She wanted to hurl the magazine at his thick,

stubborn skull. "That's your attitude for everything, isn't it? Stick your head in the sand. Ignore a problem and it'll go away. Exactly how has that worked out for you so far?"

He unfolded himself from the rug and stood.

She glowered. "Where are you going?"

"I'm starting Oliver's bath."

"And there goes your second method of dealing with anything hard." She tossed the magazine aside and got off the couch. "You run away."

He scowled. "Deploying to a conflict zone isn't running away."

"Taking a job on the opposite side of the state to bypass dealing with things you'd rather avoid is running away."

His scowl could have curled her hair. "Leaving Truelove is about making a new life for Olly."

"Oliver already has a life here." She wrapped her arms around herself. "Stop hiding behind your son."

"Mommy..." Olly whimpered.

Colton raked his hand over his head. "Now is neither the time nor the place to have this conversation."

She threw out her hands. "Then when?"

He pinched the bridge of his nose. "Tomorrow."

"We're going to the town picnic tomorrow."

Memorial Day observances would begin with a wreath-laying ceremony on the square at the statue for the Truelove war dead. Later that day, the town sponsored the much-anticipated annual mountain meadow picnic at the nearby national park.

He jammed his hands in his jeans. "Afterward then."

She nodded. "The picnic and games will finish late afternoon. I hate to bother Aunt EJ when she already does so much for Olly, but I'll ask if she would take him home with her for a few hours."

"Play the newlywed card." His mouth twisted. "She'll probably jump at the chance."

"So we'll talk through everything then?"

"Fine. Tomorrow." He headed down the hall. "Whatever you want."

Their situation was far from fine. Her stomach tanked. Nothing about this was what she wanted.

Not even close.

Monday was a perfect day for the picnic. Sunny. Warm. Blue skies. Totally unlike the storm brewing between her and Colton.

The picnic was a leashed dog–friendly event. When it was time to go, Blue jumped into the backseat of the truck and settled next to Oliver.

Blue would enjoy the chance for a supervised romp with his canine pals. The happy companionship of the large border collie and Mrs. Desmond's little Chihuahua was a funny sight to behold. Friendships sometimes sparked in the most inexplicable of hearts.

Case in point, in hers and Colton's.

The drive over the mountain to the park should

have been lovely. Around every bend, the white laurel and flame-orange azaleas were at their peaks. But the effect was lost on her.

She hated conflict. It made her feel queasy. And jittery. But this push-pull thing had to end. It wasn't fair to any of them, especially Oliver. She needed—she deserved—to know exactly where she stood with Colton.

They both needed clarity about their feelings. She fisted her hands at her side, pressing her nails into her palms. Even if the truth hurt, one way or the other, she aimed to get it.

Colton parked alongside the other vehicles in the gravel lot. A trailhead led to the picnic shelter in the meadow. Ethan waved as he and Amber headed with their kids into the trees.

"Go bear hunt, Mommy." Olly pointed to the woods.

"No bear hunt, Oliver." She undid the car seat harness and lifted him out. "We're going on a picnic today."

Tail wagging and his tongue hanging out, the border collie circled them, but stayed close. More vehicles arrived. A steady stream of people headed for the meadow.

Colton grimaced. "Looks like the whole town is here."

She set Olly on his feet. "Truelove is a tight-knit community. Most people would consider that a positive in their lives."

He bristled. So did she. They were both spoiling for an argument. And the sooner the better, in her opinion. If he wanted a fight, for the love of mousse she'd give him one.

She was tired of being his fake wife. Over the years of their friendship, she'd made it entirely too convenient for him to avoid other relationships. And look where that had landed her.

"Hey, you two! Everything okay?"

Sam, Lila and their daughter, Emma Cate, strolled toward them. Blue licked Oliver's face. Emma Cate giggled.

Mollie clipped a leash onto Blue's collar. "Everything's great."

Lila's gaze wavered between them. "Are you sure?"

Colton folded his arms. "We're fine."

Sam exchanged a look with his wife. "Can I help carry any of the food?"

"I've got it." Colton hefted the picnic basket out of the truck. "Where to?"

"Tables are set up in the meadow." Lila motioned toward the woods. "A five-minute walk along the trail."

Carrying the basket, Colton led the way. Sam kept him company on the path.

Lila favored Olly with a smile. "Would you hold Emma Cate's hand while we walk to the picnic shelter?"

Emma Cate patted Olly's head.

Oliver gave her a big smile. "Hey, Em Cay."

Lila and Mollie followed the children.

"Won't be long now." Mollie glanced at her friend, puffing with exertion at the slight incline on the trail. "And I'm not only talking about getting to the picnic."

"Six weeks," Lila wheezed. She touched her protruding belly. "Can't come soon enough for me. I can't wait to meet the newest member of Team Gibson, and I'm looking forward to seeing my feet again."

Mollie laughed. The tangy scent of evergreens filled the air. Taking a deep, cleansing breath, she resolved to make the most of the day in the great outdoors.

Colton laid the basket on one of the unoccupied picnic tables.

Despite dreading the looming confrontation, she and Colton had to talk. She couldn't go on any longer with the unresolved emotional landmine of the kiss laying between them. Handing him Blue's leash, she left Colton to watch over Olly.

On the long table under the shelter bulging with food, she unpacked her contributions to the community potluck.

Colton and Blue joined her. "We certainly won't go hungry."

"No one ever does." She set her deviled egg platter beside CoraFaye Dolan's locally famous potato salad. "Where's Oliver?"

Colton curled his hand around Blue's leash. "He's with Shayla and Jeremiah, waiting his turn at the pony ride. I'll head back in a sec."

He dropped his gaze to the pine needle-strewn ground. "For me, Memorial Day doesn't bring to mind picnics, but faces of soldiers I once knew."

Something pinged inside her chest. "I'm sorry. I should have realized."

In classic Colton fashion, he shrugged off his obvious emotion. "It's okay. You weren't to know."

She set the coconut cake—her grandmother's recipe—onto the separate dessert table. "One of us will need to walk Olly around on the pony. He's never sat on a horse. I'm not sure he'll like it."

"I'd be happy to oblige." Colton made a wry face. "If he'll let me."

She reached for Blue's leash. "If not, we'll walk with him together."

Jack Dolan, who owned the nearby equestrian center, had set up a ring of ponies to entertain the children. Included was the little Chincoteague pony that once belonged to his daughter.

Liddy's tragic death had nearly spelled the end for her parents' marriage, but with God's help and Truelove's support, Jack and Kate found their way back to each other last summer. Theirs was a love story that inevitably brought tears to her eyes.

A reminder that with God, nothing was impossible. Like her complicated situation with Colton.

He looked at her. "After the picnic, we'll talk through this, Molls. I promise."

Ambling over to stand with his son, Colton struck up a conversation with Jake McAbee of Apple Valley Orchard and his son Micah.

It gave her no end of joy to realize—whether Colton himself did or not—the former foster kid and self-labeled misfit had made a place for himself in Truelove.

A breeze ruffled his hair. Her heart turned over. Yeah, she absolutely had it bad. If only he would feel the same about her.

For a split second, a dark cloud of trepidation threatened to rob her of the joy of the day. But his words reassured her that despite his initial resistance, he cared about her concerns.

Typical Colton, though. He had to process everything first before he was ready to talk.

Aunt EJ found her at the picnic table where she'd stashed Oliver's backpack.

"Let me tend to Blue." Her great-aunt held out her hand for the leash. "You enjoy the day with your guys."

If only they really were her guys in every sense of the word.

"Thanks, Aunt EJ." She led Blue to a spot at the end of the table in the shade. "Stay, Blue."

She joined Colton and Olly just as the next pony became available.

At first, the little boy wanted only her to go with him, but she held up her phone. "I have to take your picture, sweetie pie. You want to ride the pony, don't you?"

His eyes flicked to the pony. "Horsie."

"If you want to ride the pony, let Daddy help you."

He frowned, but he raised his arms.

Colton lifted his son onto the Shetland pony's broad back.

Oliver grinned. "Me high up, Mommy."

"So high. So big," She adjusted the camera focus on her cell. "You and Daddy smile." She took the photo.

"Wrap your hands around the saddle horn, son." Colton adjusted Olly's grip and placed his own hand protectively on the small of the child's back.

Once the entire group of children was mounted, Jack walked the lead pony forward. When the Shetland pony moved underneath him, Oliver's eyes became enormous. "M-M-Mommy?"

"You're doing great, sweetie." She waved. "What a big boy you are, riding the pony."

"Mommy?" Hanging on to the saddle horn for dear life, he threw her a panicked look. The pony clip-clopped around the circle. "Me fall?"

"Daddy won't let anything bad happen to you, Olly. I promise."

After a few minutes, Oliver relaxed. By the time his turn ended, he wore a big smile. Colton plucked him off the pony. For a second, he clasped his son in his arms. An all-too-precious occurrence Oliver rarely allowed his father.

Her heart melted at the look on Colton's face.

Too soon, though, the little boy bucked, ready to be set down. When his sneakers touched the ground, he dashed toward her. "Me ride horsie, Mommy."

She gave him a quick hug. "Daddy and I are so proud of you."

They stopped to check in with Aunt EJ and Blue. Her great-aunt insisted they get something to eat.

"Good dog," Mollie praised Blue.

Olly hugged his canine best friend's neck. Colton filled Blue's doggie bowl with water.

Under the shelter, she carried Olly in her arms so he could see what was on the table and make his food selections. Oliver had always been a good, healthy eater.

Colton juggled their plates and they soon relieved Aunt EJ, who headed off to help Amber with her kids. Mollie settled the little boy on the wooden bench. Her parents joined them.

She was thrilled to see her mom out and about. The sunshine and fresh air were good for her. She couldn't remember the last time she'd seen her mother so animated.

"I've been cooped up far too long," her mom told everyone who stopped by to wish her good test results next week. "Time to get back to living life."

A niggle of worry about her mom's pending scan fretted at the edge of her mind, but today was a day made for happiness. No unhappy thoughts allowed. She sneaked a glance at Colton, talking permits and inspections with her dad.

Her stomach knotted. She put down her fork. At a nearby table, Kate Dolan laughed at something Jack said.

The Dolans were a perfect example of how God

excelled at making something beautiful out of the broken.

Dear God, please make something beautiful out of the mess Colton and I have made.

After lunch, Maggie Hollingsworth, director of the recreational center, and other volunteers supervised the old-fashioned children's games.

In the meantime, the competition was fierce during the always-hilarious tug-of-war between the police and fire departments.

There was much good-natured ribbing between team captains Police Chief Bridger Hollingsworth and Fire Chief Will MacKenzie, who were also close friends.

In the clearing, she kept a tight grip on Oliver. Thanks to an unusual infusion of sugar, courtesy of a frosted cupcake her father sneaked him, the little boy was especially squirrelly. Along with her parents and Colton, they watched from the sidelines. Sitting between them, Blue barked with excitement.

Colton cheered on Luke in the tug-of-war. Yet another friend he'd made since returning to town. She was ever so hopeful that the more ties binding him to the community, the more likely he would decide to stay in Truelove.

Amid much applause, the fire department emerged as the winners. Last year, the police department had taken the honors.

Olly strained against her hold on his hand. "Go with kids, Mommy."

"The games are for the big kids, sweetie pie."

He struggled forward, almost yanking her off her feet. "Me big kid!"

"Let the boy have fun," her father said.

"This is your fault." She shot her dad a stern look. "You and that cupcake."

Entirely unrepentant, her father grinned.

"I don't want him to get hurt."

"Stop Mollie-coddling the boy." Laughing at his own joke, her father nudged Colton. "What say you, Dad?"

Colton folded his arms. "As long as there's no blood or broken bones."

Her father nodded. "Exactly."

"Ted and I will watch Olly." Her mother smiled. "Why don't you and Colton enjoy yourselves for a bit?"

She chewed her lip. "A sugared-up Oliver can be a lot, Mom."

Three-year-old Parker called Olly over to the preschool-friendly pool noodle obstacle course.

Oliver jerked at her hand. "Mommy!"

Her mother waved her hand. "Let him play."

Against her better judgment, she let go. Surging forward, he took two steps and did a face-plant.

Wincing, she was by his side in an instant. "Olly, sweetie?"

His mouth puckered.

Colton frowned. "Don't make a big deal of it. Children fall down." He took hold of Oliver's shoulder. "You're fine, aren't you, son?"

The child's gaze swung from Mollie to his father.

"Shake it off." He helped Oliver to his feet. "You're fine."

Parker called to him.

Colton squeezed his shoulder. "Go on then."

Olly threw a last glance at her before running toward the band of children. She started to follow.

Colton caught her arm. "Your parents said they'd watch him. Stop being so overprotective."

"What you call overprotective, I call good parenting."

"Your overreaction makes him fearful. And teaches him to doubt himself." His nostrils flared. "Good thing his dad is here now. He could use toughening up."

Her mouth fell open. "He's a baby."

Colton squared his jaw. "He's not a baby. He's—"

"Ted?" Her mother pulled at her husband. "Let's leave these two to hash out what constitutes good parenting." Taking Blue, they headed after Oliver.

Hands on her hips, Mollie watched Olly crawl through a pool noodle tunnel. He tried negotiating the pool noodle hopscotch area, only to trip and hit the grass.

Mollie gasped.

"Stop with the helicoptering." Colton towed her toward the deserted picnic area. "You wanted to talk. Here's your chance."

Mollie kept her eyes peeled for Oliver. "But—"

"I shouldn't have kissed you."

She stiffened.

"What else is there to talk about?" He scuffed

the toe of his boot in the dirt. "I don't know what you want me to say."

She crossed her arms. "I want you to tell me the truth."

He rubbed the back of his neck. "I don't want to hurt you, Mollie."

"Just tell me how you feel. About me. About us. About kissing me."

He plowed his fingers through his hair. "If you must know, I regret kissing you."

She flinched.

He glared. "Are you happy now?"

She lifted her chin. "You didn't kiss me like you had regrets."

"I was feeling vulnerable and lonely. You caught me off guard. It was a mistake, Mollie. A mistake that should've never happened."

He couldn't have found a more perfect way to hurt her. Touching on every one of her insecurities. Flaying open her heart.

In that moment, Mollie—who prided herself on never losing her temper—lost it.

"You want to talk about regrets?" She jabbed her finger in his chest. He reared. "I'll tell you what's a mistake."

Her breath came in short, uneven spurts. "My biggest mistake was marrying you." Her voice rose. "You only wanted to marry me for Oliver's sake because you were being deployed."

Colton's eyes went large. She'd shocked him. Sweet, easygoing, doormat Mollie. But she was sick of being a pushover. And she told him so. At the top of her lungs.

His gaze flicked over her shoulder. "Mollie..."

She was sick of him not seeing her. Never really seeing her. She should've lowered her voice, but she couldn't stop. Not once she'd begun.

"My second biggest mistake has been pretending how happily married and in love we are when all you ever wanted from the start was to take Olly and get as far away from me and this town as you could," she shouted.

Her fury spent, she slumped against the table. But as her words echoed in the air, there came to her a slow, dawning awareness. In the space of a single heartbeat, several awful realizations became painfully apparent.

First: their raised voices had drawn a crowd. Including her horrified parents.

Stunned into silence, a significant number of Truelove citizens, including most of her friends, gaped at her.

Second: despite her pains to guard the true nature of her non-relationship with her married-for-convenience spouse, she'd declared what she'd gone to such elaborate lengths to avoid.

Humiliated within an inch of her life, she prayed for the earth to open up and swallow her. Rigid with embarrassment, Colton wore the closed-off, shutdown expression she knew too well. He was angry with her.

Good. Because she was livid with him. But more so with herself.

Her heart thudded. Maybe it wasn't as bad as she thought. How much of her rant had everyone overheard?

She caught Shayla's eye. Her petite friend gave her a sympathetic shake of her head.

Okay, so maybe it was as bad as she feared. Taking a shuddery breath, she braced for the fallout. Which promised to be cataclysmic.

She needed to apologize to everyone. Then, do her best to make amends to those she'd hurt.

Mollie had not only disgraced herself but her parents, too. Shock and disappointment were writ large across her mother's pale features. Aunt EJ and the rest of the Double Name Club appeared more sad for her and Colton than surprised.

But her father looked furious. When he took a step forward, Colton placed himself between her and her dad.

"No, Ted." Her mom put a restraining hand on his arm. "Not like this."

She could hardly bear to look at her mother. Crying, her mom appeared ready to collapse.

Then came a sudden realization—the most terrifying of them all.

"Olly?" She scanned the crowd. "Where's Olly?"

Colton's gaze swung. "Has anyone seen my boy?"

Jumping into action, Jonas Stone and nine-year-old Hunter moved about making inquiries. Luke and Shayla, too.

"Oliver?" Mollie called.

The children were still at the games in the clearing. She was grateful Oliver hadn't witnessed her total public meltdown. Yet a tiny worm of worry niggled its way into her heart.

Colton strode toward her parents. "We left him with you. He's supposed to be with you. You said you would watch him."

Some of the anger dimmed from her father's face. "We heard Mollie's voice..." He looked at his wife, at Mollie and finally at Colton. "We ran over here, worried something had happened. We believed he was with us."

Her mom sagged. "We didn't think. When we thought Mollie was in trouble, we just reacted." She put a trembling hand to her mouth. "I'm so sorry."

There was no time for recriminations. Finding Olly was her priority. Pushing past everyone, Mollie raced toward the clearing.

"Oliver!" she shouted.

Maggie Hollingsworth broke away from a group of children. "What's happened?"

It was all Mollie could do not to give into tears. "We can't find Olly. Is he with you?"

The recreational director shook her head, setting her brown ponytail aquiver. "We finished the preschool games about ten minutes ago. The older children stayed for the relay race. We sent the younger ones back with their families."

Mollie searched the crowd, hoping to catch sight of the child she loved more than life.

But there were so many people milling about. Latching on to her fear, other parents gathered their children closer. The clearing buzzed with activity.

Panning the meadow for the little boy, she spotted Jake and Callie's children. Kara and the fire chief's son Maddox.

Emily Jernigan and the doctor had a firm grip on their grandson, Jeremiah. AnnaBeth cradled a sleeping baby Violet. The Hollingsworth boys were with their police chief father.

There was no sign of Olly.

Growing dismay clawed its way from her stomach to her heart. "Oliver!" she yelled.

With Parker perched on her hip and the ten-year-old twins by her side, Amber rushed over. "We'll help you find him. He's got to be here somewhere."

But Olly wasn't there. They couldn't find him. Somehow, he had managed to slip away unnoticed. Where was he?

He wasn't the only missing child. Sam and Lila couldn't locate Emma Cate, either.

Clutching her swollen belly, Lila rushed around the meadow, searching for her daughter. Frantic, Sam was clearly torn by concern for his wife and for his little girl.

Mollie's initial agitation gave way to full-blown panic.

Just then, a disheveled Emma Cate stumbled out of the thick, canopied forest. With bits of twigs stuck in her blond braids, it appeared as if the eight-year-old had fallen down. Her knee was bleeding and leaves clung to her face. She was crying.

Sam and Lila rushed forward. "We've been so worried."

"I'm so glad you're safe." Mollie hurried over. "Have you seen Olly?"

The child's lower lip trembled. "I told him not to go into the woods by himself, but he said he and Blue were going on a..." Her brow creased. "A bear hunt?"

"Oh, no," Colton murmured.

Mollie put her hand to her throat.

"Blue barked at a squirrel. Olly ran after him. I chased them, but my side started to hurt." She pressed a hand to her ribs.

Colton knelt in front of Emma Cate. "Could you show us where you were in the forest?"

The child shook her head. "I don't know. They disappeared into the trees. I couldn't see the meadow anymore. I was lost, too."

Emma Cate began crying in earnest. Tears rolling down her own cheeks, Lila stroked the child's head.

Rising, Colton shared a long look with Mollie. "Oliver couldn't have gotten far."

Yet she sensed his words were aimed more at comforting her than something he truly believed.

Grim-faced, the police chief took charge. "We'll find him." Then he radioed for reinforcements.

Chapter Ten

Much later when twilight descended, there was still no sign of Oliver or Blue. The police chief called a halt to the search.

Mollie clutched Bridger's arm. "We can't stop looking."

"I *won't* stop looking," Colton growled.

A big man, Bridger scrubbed his hand over his face. "We're losing the light. It's going to be dark soon."

"We can't leave him out here all night." Mollie twisted her hands together. "We have to keep searching."

"The search will continue." Bridger feathered a hand through his regulation-cut dark hair. "The park rangers and every man that can be spared from Truelove will be out here at daybreak."

Colton tightened his jaw. "I won't leave without my son."

Bridger's features hardened. "You don't know the terrain. You go stumbling about in pitch-blackness, you could find yourself falling into the gorge. How would that help Olly? Last thing Mollie needs is to lose you, too. I'll have to waste time and resources rescuing you, instead of focusing on your son."

Colton had never felt so helpless in his life. He hated feeling helpless. But the police chief was right.

Mollie clung to Colton. She was at the end of her tether. Until the sun rose again, there was nothing to be done for Oliver, but she needed him now more than ever. She was barely holding it together.

"Okay..." He swallowed past the boulder in his throat. "We'll go home."

"No," she moaned.

"Just until sunrise." He hugged her close. "Then we'll be back to look for our boy." He shot Bridger a look. "If you hear anything overnight... If there are any new developments..."

Bridger gave him a short, curt nod. "I'll call you right away."

She gripped Colton's arm. "We can't give up on him."

"We're not." As Bridger made the call to suspend the search and rescue operation until morning, Colton steered her toward the trailhead. "You and I will be out here at first light, but after we get some rest first."

The hardest thing he'd ever done in his life was walk away. It took everything in him not to give into the desperate desire to rush headlong into the woods again. To keep looking until he had his son in his arms.

On the path to the parking lot, it felt like they passed nearly everyone they knew and many they didn't. A gauntlet of well-wishers for Olly to be safely restored to those who loved him most. Young and old. Men and women. Those who'd answered their plea for help.

As a result of their unexpected marriage bombshell, he glimpsed speculation on some faces. Not that he cared about any of that right now. But mostly, he beheld compassion.

Their fellow searchers fell in step behind them. The sincerity of their support washed over him. They literally had his back. Despite his fatigue and the despair that gnawed at his gut, he was incredibly touched.

She'd been right about Truelove. It was the kind of town whose residents cared for and took care of their own. Which now included Oliver. And him.

A mind-boggling concept. The sense of belonging was a feeling he'd experienced only with his brothers in arms in the Army.

Most of the younger women had long since returned to town to see to the needs of their own children. ErmaJean and IdaLee were keeping vigil with Mollie's parents. He prayed Glenda hadn't suffered a relapse.

As a measure of his gratitude, he shook the hand of each man as they wended their way out of the forest. Jake. Ethan. Jonas. Sam. Luke. Zach and his entire pit crew.

Will MacKenzie. Mayor Watkins. Clay McKendry and the cowboys at the Bar None Cattle Ranch. Jack Dolan.

Jack's wife, Kate, caught Mollie's hand. "We'll find him."

With a small cry, Mollie went into the nurse-midwife's arms. "Thank you for helping us search."

If anyone knew what they were going through, it was Jack and Kate. He couldn't imagine what it must have cost the Dolans to be here for them. What hollow memories of pain and loss this situation must have triggered in Kate and her husband.

He extended his hand to Jack. "Thank you for standing with us."

"We're going to find your boy. He's going to be okay." The former Navy SEAL pounded his chest. "I feel it in here. Don't lose heart. Keep the faith."

But faith wasn't something Colton had ever possessed in abundance.

Reaching the graveled parking lot, everyone dispersed to retrieve their vehicles. With an air of grim determination, GeorgeAnne stood beside his truck.

He stiffened. The matchmaker would have a lot to say about their marital deception. One of her sons, waiting nearby, threw him a commiserating look. A grandson of hers gave him a small thumbs-up.

There wasn't much he could do about deflecting a force of nature like GeorgeAnne Allen. Better to let her have her say and be done with it. He deserved everything she could throw at him. But he'd be hog-tied and barbecued before he let her light into Mollie.

He inserted himself between Mollie and the older woman. “We never started out to deceive anyone.” He held up his hands. “We just didn’t think through the consequences—”

“None of that matters now.” GeorgeAnne fluttered her hand. “My only concern is for Oliver.” Her face became stricken. “And for you.”

In the fading light of dusk, GeorgeAnne looked as old as he’d ever seen her. She turned toward Mollie. “For Oliver’s mother, too.”

Mollie choked out a sob. He pulled her into his arms.

“Bleak as you’re feeling—” GeorgeAnne lifted her chin “—I encourage you to not let go of your hope or each other.”

“Hard to feel much faith or hope right now,” he rasped.

Surprising him, GeorgeAnne patted his arm. “You’ve got friends to remind you. We’ll be praying without ceasing all through the night.”

He’d believed he’d never need another friend besides Mollie. Turned out he did.

“Thank you, Miss GeorgeAnne.”

Eyes suspiciously moist, she swiped a bony finger under the rim of her glasses. Probably just a trick of the dying light. GeorgeAnne was a tough old bird.

She gave him a tiny shove. “Get that girl of yours home. Try to rest some. Dinner is waiting for you.”

Trust GeorgeAnne to have thought of everything.

By the time they reached the house, night had

fallen. Someone had come and gone. A lamp glowed inside the living room. Wearily, they climbed the porch steps. There was no Blue to greet them. Most importantly, no little boy to break the unnatural stillness.

He raked his hand through his hair. "I can get you a plate of whatever was brought."

Mollie sank onto the sofa. "I'm not hungry. Are you?"

Shaking his head, he sat beside her. "No."

Her gaze darted about the room. "I've misplaced my phone."

Colton felt a tremendous need to touch her, if only the side of his jeans brushing hers.

She clenched her fist. "How can this be happening? How could I lose Olly?" Her voice rose. "I should've never taken my eyes off him. If only—"

"Don't do this to yourself," he said. "The what-ifs, the if-onlys will eat you alive. After Erin died… Then losing buddies…"

He spotted the black backpack. Someone had found it and set it against the brick of the fireplace. Last time he'd seen it, it was on the picnic table.

After rummaging through the backpack, he held the device aloft. "Your phone isn't lost forever. And neither is Oliver."

She tapped the cell but it remained black. She let out a sigh of frustration.

"No worries." He plugged it into the charger on the side table. "Just needs a little juice."

"Your phone is still working, right?" She bit her

lip. “In case Bridger tries to contact us. Or Mom and Dad.”

He dug his phone out of his pocket. “It’s good. I’ll charge yours then plug in mine.” He cocked his head. “Was there someone you wanted to call?” He handed her his phone.

“I’d rather keep the line free.” But she opened the weather app. “I want to check tonight’s low temperature.” She put her hand to her mouth. “Oh, no…”

Colton grabbed the cell. It wasn’t good news. His chest squeezed. Typical spring mountain weather, the temperature would fall into the thirties overnight.

“He’s all alone. He’ll be so cold.”

Colton’s heart wrenched. “He’s not alone. He has Blue. Olly was wearing jeans. Sneakers. A long-sleeved shirt and his jacket.”

“It’s not enough,” she whispered.

They’d grown up in these mountains. They’d been taught to respect it, too. The weather wasn’t the only potentially deadly hazard.

While the Blue Ridge was full of unsurpassed beauty, there were also venomous snakes, bobcats and black bears. And his son was lost out there in the wilderness.

A sick fear churned in his gut.

“Olly doesn’t like the dark.” She clasped her hands under her chin. “He’ll be scared and crying for me. He won’t understand why I don’t come.”

Her tortured gaze bored into Colton. “I can’t bear

for Olly to think I don't love him. I've always been there for him. I've always protected him."

Taking her in his arms, Colton held her tight. She sobbed against his shoulder. For the first time in his life, he prayed out loud to a God that, until that moment, he wasn't sure he believed in.

Entrusting Olly to his faithful Father-Creator, Colton prayed for his son to be safe and warm. For peace for all of them. For wisdom. For strength. For guidance to the right path that would lead them to his son.

Through the long, hard, sorrowful night, he and Mollie held on to each other. He'd never been a man of many words. But that night, he used them all up and then some.

As he prayed, her sobs quieted. Exhausted and utterly spent, she fell asleep. He kept vigil for both of them. It was still dark when he heard the sweet, rapturous trill of a songbird. The first fingers of gray speared the darkened sky.

Gently, he shook her awake. "Molls… Darlin', it's almost daybreak. If I leave now, I can be at the command post by dawn."

She came awake so suddenly she startled him. "I'm coming with you. Don't leave me."

He suspected—despite his previous words to the contrary—leaving her on a permanent basis might prove impossible. And if at the close of the day, Oliver wasn't found safe…

Colton sucked in a breath. He wouldn't go there. Hope. Faith. He entrusted himself, Mollie and Olly once again to the One who'd always loved them the most and the best.

Once more, they set off on the winding mountain road. He barreled into the parking lot. The tires spun gravel as he jerked to a stop. Golden streaks of pink and apricot lightened the sky. Hand in hand, they raced through the forest. The meadow had become command central.

Bridger and nearly the entire population of Truelove were already waiting.

She blinked rapidly. "Oh, my..."

His eyelids stung. The kindness of Truelove almost undid him.

"We've assigned volunteers to teams." Bridger wheeled to the large map of the national forest spread out on the table. "We'll pick up where we left off."

The K-9 search unit headed out with their handlers. The teams dispersed to their designated grids.

He and Mollie found themselves in Bridger's group. They walked abreast at carefully spaced intervals. The terrain was rugged. The undergrowth in the Southern Appalachians was lush and difficult to navigate. As they pushed obstacles out of their way, branches sometimes whiplashed them in the face.

Brambles caught and tore at their clothing. They batted away the swarming insects. There were ravines to traverse.

His heart pounded like a drumbeat in his chest. An urgency drove him to hurry. *Hurry. Hurry.*

Keeping his head on a swivel like he'd been trained, he scanned the immediate surroundings for any sign or clue the little boy had passed this way. Looking for something that didn't belong. Anything out of place. He calculated they'd come at least five miles from the meadow.

How could a small child have wandered this far? Had they missed a vital clue? Were they searching the wrong area?

"Olly. Oliver. Son," he called. Inside his head, he called out to his God. His Protector and Father.

Breathing heavily due to the altitude and steep ascent, Mollie stumbled over a fallen log.

He threw out a hand. "Are you all right?"

"I'm fine." Shaking him off, she gave him an exasperated scowl. "Olly is the only one who matters here."

That wasn't true. Had never been true. He couldn't imagine a world—a life—that didn't contain her.

Like her mama, though, she was a warrior. Fierce in her love. She wouldn't stop until they found Oliver.

And after they found Olly, he wouldn't stop until he had made everything right for her. No matter what it took. No matter what the sacrifice.

"Oliver!" she yelled. "Blue!"

In the distance, a dog barked.

They looked at each other. "Was that—?"

"It's got to be Blue," he shouted, surging forward. “Come on, Blue,” he hollered. “Do it again. Let us know where you are!”

A frenzy of excited barks erupted near an outcropping of granite boulders.

“Blue?” she screamed.

They took off at a run. With his longer legs, he quickly outpaced her.

Ears up and tail raised, the dog stood alert and vigilant in front of the rock.

“Blue!” He raced toward the border collie. “Where’s Olly?”

“Daddy?” From behind the dog came a tremulous voice. “Daddy...”

“Olly?” His heart lodged in his throat. “Son?”

Blue’s agitated barking turned into happy yips. The dog moved aside, and Colton caught his first glimpse of his child.

Oliver’s face was dirty. His clothes mud-stained and worse for wear, but never had Colton beheld a more wonderful sight than his son, alive and seemingly well.

Colton dropped to his knees. “Oliver.”

His hands clenched and unclenched at his sides, aching to hold his son, but the boy would want only Mollie.

“Olly!” She reached for him, but Oliver headed straight for Colton.

“Me wost, Daddy,” he sobbed. “Me know you find me.” He ran into Colton’s open arms.

He crushed the child to his chest. Tears ran down his cheeks. *Thank You, God. Thank You so much.*

Bridger and the others stood back to allow them their much-anticipated reunion.

Through tears of relief, she smiled at Colton. “Oliver called you ‘daddy.’”

It was as if the heavy chain dragging Colton down these last few weeks fell away into nothingness.

He took a quavery breath. “I—I guess he did.” His heart felt as light as a feather. As if he could float up into the sky and soar above the mountain peaks.

Olly turned in his arms. “Mommy!” He reached for her, but to Colton’s joy, his son kept one arm firmly entangled around his father’s neck.

She pressed into the child, who buried his face into her hair. She murmured endearments, bits of nonsensical things that made sense to his son. Olly nestled into her, while keeping his hold on his dad.

Colton wrapped his free arm around Mollie. Drawing her into their hug. They had faked their marriage of convenience. Their family, however, had become real.

She plucked a leaf caught in Oliver’s hair. “Are you all right? We’ve been so worried about you.”

“Me sad, but Bwoo keep me safe.”

Bridger nodded. “The dog probably saved his life by keeping him warm during the night.”

Colton let go of Olly to hug Blue. “Aren’t you a good boy? My hero. Thank you for taking care of Oliver, Blue.”

She stroked the dog's head. "He's the best dog ever."

Bridger got on the radio to let everyone know Oliver had been found. The search teams were recalled. Mollie insisted Olly drink from her water bottle. Colton made sure Blue got his fair share of water, too.

With Oliver perched on his shoulders, he took Mollie's hand and followed Bridger toward the central command post. Trotting along, Blue took point. In the meadow, they found everyone already assembled, waiting to celebrate Oliver's return. The search and rescue teams broke into applause.

With much backslapping for a job well done, the teams packed up the command post. Park rangers, law enforcement and the at-large residents of Truelove gathered for a well-deserved late breakfast at the picnic shelter, courtesy of Kara MacKenzie, Trudy and her culinary crew at the Mason Jar.

An EMT squad arrived. Luke checked Olly out thoroughly, much to the little boy's displeasure.

"Hungwy, Mommy."

"Give the kid some food." Luke grinned. "I'd prefer Doc Jernigan do a full workup on him, but I think other than maybe mild dehydration, he's fine. Praise God."

Praise God, indeed.

Colton wanted nothing more than just to get his boy home. After thanking the searchers once again, he buckled Oliver into his car seat. Mollie crawled into the backseat with Blue and Olly. His son babbled happily for a few minutes, but his eyes were soon drooping.

Driving down the mountain into town, within Colton, thankfulness warred against a profound understanding of his own culpability in a situation that could have so easily ended in tragedy but for the grace of God.

Humbled and contrite, he knew what he had to do. But knowing the right thing didn't make the doing of it any easier.

At the house, he pulled up next to Ted's truck. Mollie's parents waited for them on the porch. His heart twisted. The reckoning could be put off no longer. Now that the news about the real reason for their hasty marriage was out, he deserved their anger.

"I was going to call them once we got Oliver settled. Of course, they want to see for themselves he is well." She leaned forward from the back seat. "But I hadn't counted on facing them so soon."

No point in putting off the inevitable. Better to get it over with.

Colton let Blue out of the truck. Mollie climbed out after the dog. Despite his dread of the coming encounter, it did his heart good when Oliver held out his arms for his daddy to take him.

He unbuckled the straps and lifted Olly out of his car seat. No matter what the future held, he would do everything in his power to safeguard his new relationship with his son. Being Oliver's father was a responsibility—and a privilege—he didn't take for granted.

Drowsy with exhaustion, Olly snuggled against his chest. Mollie turned to Colton. "Ready?"

Together they headed toward her parents. Blue loped around the corner of the house.

Ted helped Glenda to her feet. Clinging to the railing, she wavered for a second until she found her balance. The disappointment on her face gutted Colton. Mollie started to quake.

"Mom—"

Ignoring Mollie's outstretched hand, Glenda reached for Oliver. "Hello, sweet boy. Welcome home." She rubbed his back.

Olly lifted his sleepy head. "Wenda, me camp wike big boys." He stuck his thumb into his chest. "Me big boy."

"Not so big too fast." Glenda's voice broke. "Stay my Olly for just a while longer?"

"'kay, Wenda." Oliver gave her a tired smile. "Me miss my mommy and daddy."

"They missed you, too, baby."

Closing his eyes, Oliver lay his head on Colton's shoulder. "Sweepy, Wenda..."

Ted cupped the back of the little boy's head with his work-calloused palm. But when he dropped his hand, all traces of tenderness were gone. He skewered Colton with a glance.

Anger blazed in his eyes. "How dare you." He balled his fists. "I've never been a violent man, but if you weren't holding that precious boy right now, I'd knock you to the ground."

Colton met his gaze. "I'd deserve it."

Her father's mouth puckered like he'd tasted something sour. "What was this fake marriage of yours about?"

"I've always respected your daughter, sir. I've been sleeping in the guest bedroom."

Ted jabbed his finger at him. "You and I have a different definition of respect, Atkinson."

"It wasn't like that, Daddy." Mollie snatched her father's shirtsleeve. He shook her off. "We married because of Olly. Because Colton was about to be deployed. This has always been about Oliver."

Ted pinned Colton with a glare. "Kind of an extreme solution, when a temporary guardianship would have sufficed. Plain and simple, you took advantage of my daughter."

She sucked in a breath. "No one took advantage. Colton's wife had died. He was being sent to a war zone. He wasn't thinking straight."

Glenda sniffed. "Seems to me neither of you were thinking straight."

Colton straightened. "I never meant to hurt Mollie."

Ted snorted. "You've done nothing but hurt her. She's the real loser here. Quite the merry chase you led us on all these years." His nostrils flared. "Playing on her feelings. Until she'd do anything you asked. Never minding what was right and best for her."

In his arms, Oliver stirred.

"Keep your voices down," Glenda warned.

"Colton wanted to tell everyone the truth as soon as he returned to Truelove." Mollie's lips wobbled. "It was me who convinced him to keep up the pretense after the Double Name Club unveiled their celebration plan."

Ted's brow lowered. "You're blaming a bunch of old women for making fools out of everyone who loved you?"

Colton clenched his jaw. "That was never our intention."

"There's plenty of blame to go around." Glenda glowered at Mollie. "I'm sure my daughter was more than a willing participant in this charade."

"What exactly *was* your intention?" Ted growled. "How was this ever supposed to end?"

There was only one way this could end.

Something Colton had known since he first returned to Truelove. The Double Name Club had merely provided him with an excuse to enjoy the sense of belonging, the normalcy, of being with Mollie for as long as he could. Even if it was only pretend. But it was time—past time—to do the right thing.

He squared his shoulders. "I want to apologize for the wrong I've done to Mollie and your family, sir. This was my fault."

"It wasn't all your fault." Mollie threw out her hands. "I went into the marriage with my eyes wide open. I knew what I was getting into. Colton didn't drag me into this kicking and screaming."

Glenda tapped her finger against her chin. "Care to tell us why that is, Daughter?"

Flushing, Mollie's attention dropped to her shoes.

Ted blinked at his wife. "Did I miss something here?"

Glenda tilted a look at her daughter. "That's a conversation best tabled for later, don't you think, Mollie?"

Mollie nodded.

"What's done is done." Glenda swung to Colton. "What I want to know is what you aim to do now to fix this situation."

"I plan to rectify what I can." He gulped. "Starting with moving out of the house."

Mollie's head snapped up.

"That's the least of what you're gonna do," Ted growled.

"No, Colton. You can't," she said.

The anguish in her beautiful eyes seared him. The notion of leaving this refuge—the only true home he'd ever known—was almost more than he could bear. But it had to be done. Before another day passed.

"Now that the whole town knows we're not really married—"

"We are really married." Anger and frustration laced her voice.

He heaved a sigh. "In the eyes of the law, yes. In the eyes of God and for the right reasons, no. I won't cause you to be the object of any more gossip. You deserve better than that."

Ted narrowed his eyes. "Yes, she does."

"I'll—I'll contact an attorney." He was surprised at the pain just saying the words caused him.

Mollie closed her eyes. But not before he saw the lacerating self-doubt in her gaze. Another charge to lay at his feet.

He hated himself. He hated what he'd done to his bubbly, self-confident, warmhearted best friend. He hated how he'd wrecked their lives.

She held herself tight as if bracing for a blow. "What about Olly?"

"Oliver belongs with you. You are his mom. A boy needs his mom."

Colton's gaze flicked to the home she'd created for his son. To the life she'd built for his boy. A life he'd only dreamed of as a child himself. A life he would in no way take from Olly.

"A boy also needs his father. He won't understand why you're not here." She pursed her lips. "He belongs with you, too."

Colton sighed. "I'm not leaving Truelove. We'll work out an arrangement for him to spend time with me."

"It won't be the same."

"No, it won't." He took a deep breath. "But we'll make the best of a difficult situation. We have to. For his sake."

Her eyes welled with tears.

Colton's heart plummeted. If he didn't leave

this minute, he might never find the strength to do the right thing by Mollie again. He hadn't realized doing the right thing could be so hard. Or hurt so much.

"Take him, please." He thrust his sleeping son at her.

She held his child's head against her shoulder. "Where will you go?"

He turned on his heel. "I don't know."

"Wait. Don't you want to pack your things?"

The only thing of any real, lasting value he'd be leaving behind was her and his son.

He dared not turn around. "I'll collect them when I visit Oliver," he said, his voice gruff.

"Please don't go."

"I have to."

Mollie began to cry. Soft, hopeless sobs.

And as he drove away, his heart splintered.

Chapter Eleven

Thirty minutes after Colton drove away, Mollie leaned over the sleeping child and smoothed back a lock of Oliver's hair. After a much-needed bath, he smelled of baby shampoo and soap.

She kissed his forehead. Her throat tightened at the thought of how the situation could have ended so differently. She thanked God he was alive and well.

Mollie tucked the covers of the quilt around the little boy. Another crisis awaited her in the living room—facing her parents now that her real relationship with Colton had been revealed. The last twenty-four hours had been an emotional roller coaster. She could weep with exhaustion.

But her parents deserved an explanation. Keeping the truth from them had been inexcusable. Shayla had warned her about keeping secrets.

Mollie could hardly bear to think about Colton. She'd lost him. In every way that ever mattered. The dreams she'd only recently acknowledged lay in ruins.

He'd reverted to the boy she met on the playground that long-ago day. Before friendship and kindness and love eroded the rough edges of a childhood grounded in neglect and abandonment. She'd believed her love could erase his high-walled barricades.

Barriers once again in place, he'd reerected a shield around his heart. Reestablished the fortifications she'd spent years trying to demolish. Completely shutting her out. An unbridgeable gulf yawned between them.

Her heart heavy, she slipped out of Olly's bedroom. She leaned against the closed bedroom door. *Why, God? Why did this have to happen?*

But she already knew the answer. She and Colton hadn't gotten together for the right reasons. She'd forged ahead, thinking she knew best.

She'd been full of her own plans. Heedless of the consequences. Rushing headlong into a disaster of her own making. Now those plans were in ashes.

Perhaps if she'd turned to God first, she wouldn't have found herself in this heartbreaking mess. But the truth was that she hadn't sought His counsel because she'd been afraid He wouldn't give her what she wanted most—a happily-ever-after with the man she loved.

Instead of trusting God's best for her and Colton, she'd taken the reins of her life into her own hands. Not trusted God's best for them. Because she was afraid His best might mean "no."

Guilt and remorse broke something inside her.

I'm sorry, Father. Please show me what You would have me do now. For all our sakes.

Steeling herself, she ventured into the living room. Her parents sat together on the couch. At the sound of her steps, they looked up. Her mother's anguished face tore at Mollie.

"I'm so sorry," Mollie sobbed. "For the mess I've made of everything. For disappointing you."

Her dad pulled her to the sofa. With her parents on either side, she sank onto the couch.

Tears cascaded down her face. "I don't know where to begin to explain."

He put his arm around her. The comforting scent of his Old Spice aftershave enveloped her. "Just talk to us, Mollie girl."

She told them everything. About the teenage pact she and Colton made. About the feelings that had grown in her heart. How every path had led them back to each other. How his proposal had seemed the answer to the deepest desires of her heart.

"I was wrong to keep this from you." She held tight to their hands. "Be angry with me, but please don't be angry with him."

"There's nothing you could do that would ever make us stop loving you." Her father's voice broke. "We've loved that boy for years. Too late to stop now."

Her mother drew Mollie's head onto her shoulder. "We love you, honey. Always have. Always will."

Mollie clung to her parents. "I—I love you, too."

With their arms around her, she cried as she hadn't since she was a little girl.

Laying a paper-thin hand to her cheek, her mom peered into her eyes. "Do you truly love Colton, Mollie?"

"I—I do." There was a great sense of relief in finally saying the words out loud. "But he doesn't love me." She blinked back another round of tears.

Her father rubbed his jaw. "I wouldn't be too sure about that. I've seen how he looks at you when he thinks no one is watching."

Mollie's mother smiled. "I suspect there is more real than false about your marriage."

"He won't let me in, Mom," she whispered. "He won't allow anyone into his heart, except Oliver. Without Colton, I can't bear to think what my life will be."

Mollie's mother squeezed her hand. "What can we do to help?"

"Pray for us. Especially for Colton. As sad and confused as I feel, I have Olly, my family and friends to comfort me." Tears pricked her eyes. "He has no one."

She couldn't bear to think of him out there somewhere, lost and alone. *Please look after him, God.* Where had he gone?

A whisper of an answer flitted through her brain. Getting off the couch, she sent off a quick text to the most unlikely of allies.

Unsure where he should go, Colton drove around for a couple of hours. Aimless and unanchored. In a way he hadn't felt since…

Since a young girl with blue-gray eyes and auburn-tinted hair broke through his defenses and declared herself his friend.

Without realizing how, he found himself pulling into GeorgeAnne's midcentury brick home on the outskirts of Truelove.

Rethinking the wisdom of showing up here of all places, he was about to reverse out of the driveway when GeorgeAnne emerged from the house. She marched up to his window and rapped her knuckles on the glass.

Bracing for the tongue-lashing he deserved, he lowered the window.

Her work-roughened hands planted on her bony hips, she glowered at him through horn-rimmed glasses. "You going to sit out here all day, or come in and have lunch?"

"Lunch?"

Had it only been a few hours ago Oliver was found? So much had happened, including the confrontation with the Drakes and walking away from Mollie, he felt it ought to be far later.

"BLT okay with you?" GeorgeAnne pushed the bridge of her glasses higher onto her nose. "You always liked my BLTs when you worked Saturdays at the store. It's too early for tomatoes from my garden. Will store-bought tomatoes suit you?"

He'd come at a bad time. "I didn't mean to interrupt your lunch."

She snorted. "Haven't eaten yet. Waiting on you."

He was confused. "You made lunch for me?"

"I didn't know if you'd come." For a second, her eyes slid away from him. "But I hoped you might."

Colton blinked at her.

She turned on the heel of her sensible brown shoes. "When you come into the kitchen, wipe your feet on the mat."

He scowled. But then, he got out of the truck and followed her around the corner of the house. In Truelove, backyards were where folks did most of their living.

She slipped into the house. The screen door banged behind her. She stirred a pot on the stove.

He wiped his feet before venturing inside.

She motioned to the sink. "Hands."

"Yes, ma'am." He hurried to the sink, turned on the faucet and squirted soap in his hands.

She ladled what looked like chicken noodle soup into a green pottery bowl. "Take a seat."

After drying his hands, he pulled out a chair.

She set the bowl and a sandwich plate in front of him. "When's the last time you had something to eat?"

He cocked his head, thinking out loud. "Yesterday?"

"Been a rough twenty-four hours, hasn't it?"

He sighed. "I've endured twenty-four-hour shelling less stressful than losing Olly."

Bringing another sandwich plate, she sat across from him. "And then there was this morning."

He narrowed his eyes at her. "The Truelove

grapevine strikes again. Your spies are truly everywhere."

The Double Name Club member skewered him with a glance. "You needn't take that tone with me, Colton Atkinson. Mollie texted. She was worried you had nowhere to go. I told her I'd take care of you."

He flushed. Even when he was a total jerk, Mollie looked out for him. "What were you going to do if I hadn't shown up here?"

"I'd have sent my boys out to make sure you were okay." She waved her hand. "Your soup's getting cold. Time enough to hash through the muddle you've made after we eat. I'll say grace." She pointed her finger at him. "Bow your head."

Interfering… Bossy… He gnashed his teeth. But the soup smelled good. His stomach rumbled. He closed his eyes.

"Bless us to Thy service, O Lord, and these Your gifts, which we are about to receive from Your bounty. Through Christ our Lord. Amen."

"Amen."

While they ate, a short-lived silence reigned.

"You ate the soup like you didn't hate it." GeorgeAnne scraped her chair across the linoleum. "My boys always liked my soup. And if I know anything, it's boys. You want more?"

"Please." Sheepish, he handed over his bowl. "That would be wonderful."

She filled his bowl and returned it to him. The older woman bustled about the kitchen while he finished eating. "I do love to see a man eat. I don't hold with that peculiar, birdlike eating most girls are taught."

He carried the bowl and plate to the sink. "Thank you. I didn't realize how hungry I was."

"Not until it was put right in front of you." She rinsed his plate and handed it to him to deposit in the dishwasher. "Kind of the story of your life."

His mouth flattened. "You know nothing about my life."

"You'd be surprised what I know." She rinsed the soup bowl. "Mind how you stack my dishes. I'm sure you haven't forgotten the Allen store policy. You break it, you buy it."

Anger churned in his gut. He placed the dishes—with exquisite care—into the dishwasher. "What I remember is how hard you were on me."

She turned off the faucet. "Such a sullen, stubborn, hardheaded child. What sweet Mollie Drake ever saw in you I'm sure I don't know."

"Me, neither," he barked.

"Finally." GeorgeAnne raised her eyebrow. "One thing on which we agree."

Despite himself, he laughed. What passed for a smile flitted across her features.

She motioned toward the table. "For this next bit, let's sit down again, shall we?"

"What next bit?"

She sat down. "The bit I call an intervention."

Yanking out the chair, he sank into it. "Your version of tough love, Miss GeorgeAnne?"

"It was the role that seemed to suit me best." She shrugged. "I left the love part to AnnieFrances Drake and her kin."

His brow creased.

"You were never as alone as you believed. Almost from the beginning, you were on our radar. Over the years, decades of Truelove's youngest inhabitants passed through my dear friend's elementary classroom. IdaLee was in a unique position to identify then direct our not inconsiderable talents to certain individuals in need of support, such as yourself and others."

"What others?"

She steepled her hands. "Like Sam Gibson and his mother."

His mouth twisted. "Others from the same broken-down trailer park hollow, you mean?"

"Those, who through no fault of their own, needed a little extra kindness." She laid her palms flat upon the table. "That has been the real mission of the Double Name Club for more than four decades. The point of the grapevine."

"You're telling me there's a secret Truelove society?" He gaped at her. "A conspiracy?"

The old woman rolled her eyes. "You make it sound far more dramatic than it is." She inclined her head. "We prefer to think of it as a conspiracy of encouragement. The past does not have to determine a person's future. We made sure Sam got enough word-of-mouth clients to build his paint business. He got his happily-ever-after, too."

Colton stiffened. "I was one of your little projects?"

She threw him a sharp look. "Neither you nor Sam or any of the rest were a project to be checked off on some do-gooder list. We care deeply for every individual we assist."

He grimaced. "So you gave me a job at the hardware store on weekends. And you arranged for Ted to offer me summer construction work to learn a trade?"

"That came later."

His gaze dropped to the table and her laced hands. The joints were more gnarled than he remembered. There might not be as much pep in her step, but her back remained ramrod straight.

"As much as I'd like the Double Name Club to take credit, little Mollie Drake beat us to the punch. Her friendship drew our attention to you. Her grandmother AnnieFrances became our point person on your behalf."

Something tightened in his chest. It came as no real surprise that everything good in his life could be directly traced to Mollie.

"That girl has the most loving, generous of hearts. The kind of heart that sees a need and does everything to meet it. That sees past the discarded to the potential."

He dropped his chin. "In my case, to her own detriment."

GeorgeAnne pursed her lips. "That is yet to be determined. I suspect, in a few years, Mollie Frances Drake will make a wonderful addition to the Double Name Club. AnnieFrances was a charter member. We miss her dearly."

Mollie's grandmother had been good to him. Perhaps why he'd felt so much at home in her house with Mollie and his son.

He knotted his hands in his lap. "I'm sorry for the trouble you went to on our behalf to recreate romantic milestones for an 'us' that didn't exist."

"Did you and Mollie enjoy those occasions?"

As he recalled the melted chocolate and strawberries, a smile lifted his cheeks. "We did. It was fun."

She studied him a moment. "Then it accomplished its purpose."

He frowned, unsure of what purpose she meant.

"What are your plans now that everyone knows yours is a marriage of convenience?" She perched on the edge of her seat. "Are you leaving Truelove?"

"Oliver will stay with Mollie." He scrubbed his face with his hand. "But I won't abandon my son like my parents did, if that's what you're asking."

"It wasn't." Once again all business, her tone was brisk. "You are nothing like them."

That might have been the nicest thing GeorgeAnne Allen had ever said to him. In a backhanded sort of way, of course.

"I've destroyed my relationship with Mollie's dad. I'll need to find another job."

"You enjoyed the work you did for Ted, didn't you?"

He nodded. "Maybe I can find something similar in Asheville or Boone."

"Until you get yourself sorted, I have an extra bedroom you can use."

His eyebrows rose. "You'd let me stay in your house?"

She flicked him a look. "I don't know why you continue to act so surprised when someone shows you a kindness. You're among friends in Truelove. You always have been."

"Guess I'm a slow learner."

"'Slow' isn't the word that comes to mind. Try obstinate. Or pigheaded."

He squared his jaw. "I refuse to be a charity case. I can pay my own way."

The older woman waved away his words. "Maybe you could do a few odd jobs around the house for me. The real question is, what are you going to do about your wife?"

"She's my wife in name only." He blew out a breath. "I'll contact an attorney in Asheville."

"Must you?" A furrow creased her brow. "It's as clear as the nose on your face, you two were meant to be."

"What other solution is there?"

"I can think of a much simpler one." GeorgeAnne made a disgusted noise in the back of her throat. "But you've always had to do everything the hard way. Why should this be any different?"

His cell dinged. A text from Mollie. "She wants

me to come by tomorrow morning to be there when Oliver gets up."

Colton was grateful to hear from her. When he left, she'd been so upset. As he drove around town, the memory of her sobs had torn at him. He'd wanted so much to turn around and tell her to forget everything he'd said. But a marriage in name only wasn't fair to her. She deserved far more than what he was capable of giving.

"There's some things I'd like to square away at the jobsite so Ted won't have to deal with them."

GeorgeAnne rose. "You're making a mistake in walking away from a life with Mollie."

He shook his head. He'd ruined any chance of happiness for himself. "I won't allow Mollie to suffer any further consequences from my selfish actions."

No matter what he had to do, no matter the sacrifice he had to make, he'd ensure Mollie got the happily-ever-after she deserved.

Even if it meant her happily-ever-after didn't include him.

Chapter Twelve

Bright and early the next morning, Colton arrived at Mollie's house as she'd requested. Blue's greeting was exuberant.

Having just awoken, the little boy hung on to his dad like he hadn't seen him in a decade. Despite everything else that had happened between her and Colton, Mollie was glad to see them together.

She kept her distance, allowing them the time alone to bond with each other. She let Colton take charge of making Olly's breakfast and getting him dressed.

Glancing at the clock, Colton got off the floor where he and his son were building a tower of blocks.

Oliver frowned. "Daddy work?"

"Daddy has to go to work." Colton swung his gaze to her. "I want to hand off some notes to your father about the project."

Olly tugged at each of their hands. "Go with Daddy?"

"Not today." Her eyes caught Colton's. "But

maybe your daddy could spend some time with you before bed?"

"I'd love to." He ruffled his son's hair. "See you tonight, Oliver."

A little later, she headed toward her great-aunt's house to drop off Olly with Aunt EJ.

They found her in the backyard, weeding the raised garden bed. ErmaJean's wrinkled face broke into a smile. Oliver ran to her. He loved going to EJ's house. During summer break, Mollie's great-aunt was a lifesaver for a working mom like herself.

Mollie hadn't let him out of her sight since he was found yesterday. And she was loathe to be parted from him now. Something of her thoughts must have shown themselves on her face.

"Don't worry. He'll be fine." Aunt EJ handed the child a wicker basket. "We're going to harvest the last of my strawberries this morning."

Mollie chewed her lip. "It's me I'm worried about not being fine without him."

But she needed to catch up with the appointments she'd rescheduled from yesterday, in addition to the clients already booked for today.

Having located a small trowel, he busily dug to his heart's content in an area Aunt EJ reserved for him.

Mollie squatted beside him. "I have to go now, sweetie pie."

Olly threw his arms around her neck. "Mommy, no go."

Her heart wrenched. She hated, hated, hated

leaving him like this, even with his beloved Aunt EJ. It was too soon.

Aunt EJ rested her hand on his shoulder. "Mommy has to go to work, but you and I—we're going to have a great day."

His lower lip protruded. "Mommy come back?"

Mollie kissed a tiny spot of skin below his earlobe. "I'll come back quickly as I can, I promise."

His stranglehold around her neck loosened. "Me help Gigi."

She brushed her lips across his forehead. "That's my good, dear boy."

Aunt EJ steered him to a seed starter kit on a low bench. "We've got sweet peas to plant today, young man."

Her aunt doled out one seed at a time for the child to drop into each of the pods. Suitably distracted, he loved nothing better than getting his hands in the dirt. Headed to her car, Mollie only taken a few steps when her cell dinged.

She fished her phone out of her pocket. "Mom?"

"H-honey?" Her mother's voice hitched. "The oncologist called first thing."

Suddenly lightheaded, Mollie leaned against the raised garden planter for support.

Aunt EJ placed her hand on Mollie's arm. "The scan?"

Her stomach roiling, she nodded. One way or the other, the results would change their lives forever.

ErmaJean took hold of her hand. "Faith, not fear."

Mollie held the phone between them so the older woman could hear, too.

Her mouth gone dry, she moistened her lips. "What did the doctor say, Mom?" She squeezed her eyes shut. *God, please...*

"The scans looked good." Her mother's voice wobbled. "The cancer is gone. My treatment is done."

Her aunt threw up her hands. "Praise God!"

A few seconds passed before Mollie absorbed the news everyone had been praying for.

"Honey? Did you hear what I said?"

Tears flowed down Mollie's cheeks. She put her hand to her mouth.

Aunt EJ took possession of the phone. "Glenda? It's ErmaJean. Mollie and Oliver are at my house." She put her arm around Mollie. "Yes. Yes. Everyone is fine. More than fine. We're so thrilled about your good report. It's an answer to our prayers."

Her aunt held out the phone to her. But unable to give voice to the feelings rushing through her, Mollie shook her head.

Olly tugged on her jeans. "Mommy sad?"

Crouching beside the little boy, she gathered him into her arms. "Mommy's crying because she's happy."

The child arched his eyebrow. "Mommy. Mommy. Mommy. You not cry when you not sad."

Aunt EJ chuckled. "Sounds like something his father would say."

Oliver patted Mollie's shoulder. "Me hug you, Mommy, and you feel better?"

She smiled at him. "An Olly hug always makes me feel better." She breathed in the sweet, little boy scent of him.

ErmaJean turned her attention to the phone. "Yes. We're still here. Mollie's just a bit overcome with emotion." She cocked her head at her great-niece.

Mollie swiped at her eyes. "Tell her I'm so grateful and relieved." Her voice broke. She waved her hands. "I'll call her as soon as I get to the salon."

While Aunt EJ relayed the message, Oliver returned to his "gardening."

Her great-aunt clicked off the cell. For a moment, she and Mollie looked at each other. Then Mollie threw her arms around the older woman. Like a pair of giddy teenagers, they rocked back and forth for a couple of seconds from sheer joy.

Eventually, Mollie took her leave. Between ErmaJean and the central grapevine hub at Hair Raisers, the good news would soon wend its way through Truelove.

That evening, Colton arrived to spend a few hours with Olly. "I happened to be with your dad when your mother called. I've been praying for her."

She ushered him into the house. "Thank you."

His face shone. "I'm so happy for all of you."

She did not doubt he loved her mother and her father. If only he would allow himself to love her, too.

Over the next few days, she continued to wrestle with her unrequited feelings for him. He came by mornings and evenings. But Oliver didn't understand why his father was no longer living with them.

Sometimes she'd find Olly in the empty guest bedroom. With his head on Colton's pillow, the little boy had taken to playing on the bed. Perhaps it made him feel nearer to his absent dad. It shattered her heart.

The June weather had turned sunny and warm. Colton and Oliver often spent the evening in the backyard playing games. Blue raced around. Colton rolled a large, soft ball on the ground toward Olly for the little boy to "catch."

She didn't ask, but Aunt EJ, via GeorgeAnne, kept her informed about how Colton spent his days—mainly looking for work. He'd had several interviews. He'd also scheduled an appointment with a lawyer.

Despite seeing him twice a day, their brief interactions were stiff and formal. She missed him—she missed *them*—so badly she ached inside.

Yet living apart clarified a lot of issues. It was obvious he would never see her as someone other than as a best friend, or as Oliver's surrogate mother.

Having gotten a glimpse of what true love should be, she was no longer willing to settle for anything less. Not even for Colton.

Father and son no longer needed her to act as

their go-between. Which made Mollie sad for herself but happy for their budding relationship.

She spent a great deal of time reflecting on her part in what brought them to this point. The fault lay as much within herself as with Colton.

Finally, she took her fears, her dreams and her hopes to the One she should have entrusted them to from the beginning. In the privacy of her bedroom Saturday night, she cried out the anguish in her heart. She grieved where her selfish choices had led them. Regretted the lies she'd told herself to justify doing what she wanted, instead of doing what was right.

But her faithful Creator always did what was right. He loved Colton and Oliver far more than she could love them. As she poured out her heart to Him, she surrendered her plans and her hopes to the One with whom those dreams were the safest.

Gradually, the crushing turmoil in her heart eased. An unexpected, if painful, peace prevailed. She prayed for the strength to do what she knew she must—to make this right for Colton and Olly. But doing the right thing would break her heart in two.

On Sunday evening, she met Colton at the door with her purse slung over her shoulder.

"You're going out?" He darted a glance at her car in the driveway. "Should I visit Oliver another time?"

"He's waiting for you." She took out her keys. "I'm heading to my parents for a few hours. Have fun with him. You'll need to put him to bed."

"But we always put him to bed together."

Courage, Lord. Courage.

"Not tonight." She forced a smile. "You and Olly will be fine without me."

Colton looked as if he wanted to say something, but he didn't. After a second, his gaze drifted past her. "Are Olly and Blue in the backyard?"

The unruly part of her heart pinched. Was she that easily replaced in his affections? She berated herself for being a fool. For the umpteenth time, she breathed a fresh prayer of surrender to the One who alone should be the recipient of her devotion.

Mollie found her mom and dad eating at the table on the screened porch. She rapped on the door. "Knock, knock. Am I interrupting?"

"You're never an interruption." Her father scraped back his chair. "Come in, Mollie girl. Just in time for pie."

Her mom lifted her face for a kiss. "Always wonderful to see you."

Mollie kissed her. "You're looking good."

There was a rosy glow to her mother's complexion and a sparkle in her eyes. Another coil of tension loosened from the tightness in her belly.

"That she does." Her dad winked. "Bright-eyed and bushy-tailed."

Her mom patted the chair beside her. "I'm feeling like maybe I could return to work. Just for a few hours every day until I regain my full stamina. If that would be okay with you."

"It's your business, Mom."

Her mother shook her head. "Hair Raisers is a family business. There's more than enough work if you'd like to stay. Thanks to you, Hair Raisers' clientele has grown in my absence."

Mollie's father exchanged a look with her mom. "No pressure, though. We enjoy having you here in Truelove, but if that's not what you want—"

"I can't imagine ever living anywhere else again. This is home."

Her mother released a breath. "That's what we were hoping you'd say. We'll add another salon chair. I've also been thinking about putting in a mani-pedi station."

"Really?"

Her mom smiled. "It's something I've been interested in pursuing, but being the only hairstylist in town meant there was never enough room in my schedule to give it a try. I think it's something the women in Truelove would embrace."

"Absolutely."

Her mother beamed. "It would also mean I wouldn't have to be on my feet as much. I'm not getting any younger. But thanks to the grace of God, I have been given a chance to grow older."

Mollie clutched her hand. "For which, I am grateful."

Her mother's gaze clouded. "This is an unexpected treat to see you tonight, but is something going on, honey?"

She took a quick breath. "I was wrong to keep secrets from the two people who love me the most.

I don't want to make that mistake again. If I'd come to you and God first, perhaps I wouldn't be in the predicament I find myself in now."

Her dad's face shadowed. "Had we said or done something that caused you not to trust us?"

Mollie's mother bit her lip. "I blame myself. If I hadn't been ill, perhaps—"

"No, Mom." She shot a glance between her parents. "Your illness was the convenient rationalization I used to lie to myself about why I did what I did. It was never anything to do with you. It has only ever been about my lack of trust in God."

Her father touched her arm. "I don't understand."

"I was afraid you might tell me something I didn't want to hear." Tears pricked her eyelids. "I've loved Colton for so long."

Her mother gave her a bittersweet smile. "Your father and I have known that probably before you knew it yourself."

Mollie's dad cleared his throat. "And we've loved Colton. Like a son."

Tears misted her eyes. "Thank you for always making him feel like a part of the family. He needed that in his life. More than he ever needed anything else, but God."

A crease formed between her mom's brows. "If you feared he'd never love you as anything more than a friend, I don't understand why you accepted his proposal."

"Because I wanted to be in his life so badly I didn't care what I had to do or who I had to hurt to get what I wanted most." Mollie swallowed. "I wanted him more than I wanted to do the right thing."

She dropped her gaze to her lap. "I'm so sorry for the pain I've caused you… The pain my selfishness has inflicted on Oliver…" After wading through a flood of emotion, she straightened.

"I can no longer justify keeping Colton from his son. I need to get out of their way so their relationship can grow into what God always meant it to be."

Mollie told them about the difficult decision she'd made.

Her dad scrubbed his hand over his face. "You're sure about this?"

"I don't know what the future holds, but I know who must hold my future. It's into His hands I commit those I love the most."

"You have our support no matter what." Mollie's mom teared up. "But are you sure you want to do this, honey?"

"I'm sure," she whispered. "I want you to have the chance to tell them goodbye, too."

She talked through a few logistics with them about what the next week would hold.

"I have one more stop to make before I talk to Colton. I'd prefer for Aunt EJ to get the word out about what's happening so I don't have to hash this out over and over again with everyone in Truelove."

Her father rose with her. "People will be concerned because they care about you."

The days ahead promised to be rough. "I'm going

to need their care." She took a shaky breath. "Especially those first few weeks after they're gone."

Her great-aunt took the news better than she expected. "This is not the outcome I hoped for when we came up with the idea for the milestone date nights. I'm sorry."

Mollie lifted her chin. "I'll treasure those memories forever. It was like we were dating for real. One night each week, it was a dream come true."

Aunt EJ's gaze swept her face. "Colton may not have come to terms with it, but he loves you."

"Deep down, I believe you're right." She blew out a breath. "But he won't let me love him."

"Because of his childhood, he's afraid to trust love. He's terrified of allowing himself happiness." Her aunt gave her a sad smile. "You represent everything he wants and fears the most. He's running scared."

"I can't live like this anymore, Aunt EJ. Waiting for something that is probably never going to happen. Hoping for him to get over his fears and love me. We need to get on with our lives."

She gave Mollie's hands a gentle squeeze. "I'm praying for the Lord's best for each of you. I love you, dear one."

"I love you, too, Aunt EJ."

At the house, she found Colton in the living room staring bleakly at the fireplace mantel.

Seeing him in the chair he'd claimed as his own these last few months brought lovely images of their fun-due night and other happy evenings together when she'd believed her fondest dreams were coming true. But there would be no fairy-tale ending for them.

He got out of the chair. "Is everything all right with your mom? Your dad?"

She laid her purse on the side table. "They're fine. Why do you ask?"

He shuffled his feet on the rug. "When you left, you just seemed so…"

"So what?"

His Adam's apple bobbed in his throat. "Subdued." His gaze caught hers.

Mollie's heart did the usual thump against her ribcage. One glance. That's all it ever took. *How long, Lord, before I stop feeling this way? A year? Fifteen? Never?*

Loving Colton had the hallmarks of a terminal illness. She was so tired. So tired of being in love with someone who didn't love her back. Tired of hurting.

Not sure how much longer her legs would support her, she sat on the sofa. "It's time."

His handsome brow—*for the love of curlers, stop it, Mollie*—creased. "Time for what?"

"Time to stop kidding ourselves."

He dropped into the chair. Close enough for their knees to touch. Which mustn't under any circumstances happen. Not if she hoped to say what must be said.

Shifting, she inserted space between them. A minuscule amount, yet one that gave them both more breathing room. Her movement did not go unnoticed.

"Molls?" His voice sharpened. "What's going on in that head of yours?"

"Next weekend is Father's Day." She forced herself to meet his probing gaze. "It's time to stop pretending to be something we're not. Something we won't ever be."

He sucked in a breath. "What are you saying?"

"You should take the job at the beach with Olly as you planned."

"Leave Truelove? Leave y-you?" His eyes widened. "What about us?"

She sighed. "There is no us. There never really was."

He shook his head. "You don't mean that, Molls. You can't mean that." Springing from the chair, he reached for her.

Shying away, she hurried over to the fireplace. If he touched her, she would be lost. All her good intentions would go out the window.

"Mom's health is on the rebound. You and Olly are in a good place with each other. That was our agreement."

He cleared his throat. "We've made it work this week. There's no need to take such drastic action. Your parents—"

"I've run this past my parents. Exactly what I should have done a year ago. They understand what needs to happen."

His face—those ruggedly handsome features

she'd loved for most of her life—settled into the obstinacy she knew far too well. "Make me understand why I have to uproot Oliver from everyone and everything he's ever loved."

She could be stubborn, too. Especially when it was for their own good. "Two months ago, this was what you wanted, Colton."

He jutted his jaw. "Suppose I've changed my mind?"

For a split second, a tendril of sweet hope unfurled. "Changed your mind about what?" Unable to draw a proper breath, she tensed, waiting for his answer.

He gaped at her. "I… I…"

The war erupting across his features would have been comical if it hadn't been so tragic.

His chest heaved. "Oliver and I don't have to leave Truelove. He'd be lost without you. You're the only mother he's ever known."

She would be lost without Olly. But she couldn't continue in this never-ending, non-relationship with his father.

Colton moved as if to touch her, but perhaps reconsidering, he dropped his hands. "Oliver should stay with you. I'll find another job in Truelove or close by. We can make it work. Like we always do."

"There is no making this work." She let out the breath she'd been holding. "Not this time."

His eyes pleaded with her. "We're friends, Mollie. Best friends forever."

"Our friendship—" casting her gaze around the

room, she fluttered her hands "—if that's what we truly are to each other, isn't working for me. I can't be your friend anymore, Colton."

He flinched. "Don't say that."

If she lived to be a hundred, she'd never forget the look on his face. The overwhelming bewilderment. The raw, aching vulnerability. The bitter betrayal. But she could no longer live in the realm of self-delusion.

She knotted her hands. "Why prolong the agony of the inevitable?"

If he stayed in town because of Oliver, they'd see each other daily. In a place the size of Truelove, they would likely run into each other on every corner.

She couldn't bear to be on the periphery of his life, but never in any way that meant something. She couldn't contemplate the awfulness of being near him, but never truly with him.

He crossed and uncrossed his arms. "It's been an upsetting few weeks. Once you've had time to think this through, you'll see..."

Dreadful, horrible tears hovered on the edge of her vision. *God, help me. Please. Help me to make him understand. Help me to be strong for both of us.*

She dashed away her tears. "Don't you see, Colton? If we can't be more than friends, then we can't be just friends, either."

"You can't mean that," he whispered.

With an effort of extreme will, she banished

the image of the boy sitting alone on a playground bench one long-ago day. The boy, now man, she'd loved for so long.

She took a deep breath. "If we are to survive this, I have to let both of you go." She folded her arms across herself. The gold of her wedding band glinted in the glow cast by the lamp on the side table.

"It's time to stop with the lies." Her gaze caught his and locked. "Most of all, with the lies we've told ourselves."

"Olly loves you." He clenched his teeth. "He loves it here."

"Sand, seagulls or waves…" She gave him the gentlest of smiles. "Your son will love whatever his father loves. All I ask is you give me a few days to prepare him for the transition. To say goodbye. It's better this way, Colton."

"Better for whom?" he growled.

She moistened her lips. "Better for my heart and for Olly's."

His eyes fell to her mouth. "What about my heart?"

Mollie's pulse leaped. "What about your heart, Colton?"

But he pressed his lips together and said nothing. Just as she'd supposed. Her gut twisted painfully. When would she get it through her thick skull there was no happily-ever-after for her and Colton?

Wrenching the wedding band off her finger, she held it out to him.

His eyes darkened into a stormy blue. “It belongs to you.”

“That’s just the thing, Colton.” Her voice hitched. “I don’t think it ever truly did.” She thrust it into his hand.

He left soon after. And she was glad. She wasn’t sure how much longer she could have held it together.

From the bay window, she watched the red taillights of his truck disappeared into the darkness.

Mollie turned off the table lamp.

Enfolded by the crocheted afghan IdaLee had made for Mollie’s so-called wedding, she curled into Colton’s chair. The leather held traces of his scent—a musky sandalwood and something that was just him.

A sob tore loose from her throat.

Sitting there alone in the dark, she cried herself to sleep.

Chapter Thirteen

Completely gutted, Colton drove away from the house he'd forever think of as home.

Grappling with the sudden shock of Mollie cutting him out of her life, he felt adrift. This couldn't be happening.

He stumbled into GeorgeAnne's kitchen. One look at her face and he could tell she knew what had transpired between him and Mollie.

"I'm sure you think me an interfering old woman for making you and Mollie go out on those date nights."

His gaze shot to hers. "The last two months have been the best of my life. No matter how things turned out, I'll never regret this time I've had with my boy and Mollie." Heart aching, he looked away. "It's late. I should get to bed."

"Don't give up on her, Colton."

"She's given up on me. On us. Who can blame her?"

GeorgeAnne shook her head. "I refuse to believe all hope is lost. You're going to need to fight for her."

"I—I can't talk about Mollie tonight." His voice

hitched. "How am I going to be the dad Olly deserves? How am I supposed to make a home for him?"

A belated realization slammed into him, nearly knocking the breath from his lungs. "Mollie *is* our home."

GeorgeAnne caught hold of his hand. There was a strength in her grip. "I'll help you in any way I can. You're not alone, dear boy."

"Somehow…" He inhaled. "I think I've always known that, Miss GeorgeAnne."

He shocked himself by hugging the matchmaker. At first, because she was GeorgeAnne, she stiffened. But a split second later, her arms came around him.

When she pulled away, her eyes looked moist. "Do you want to know the real reason the matchmakers do what we do?"

"You already told me. The Double Name Club's purpose is to help those who need it the most."

She shook her head. "Every one of us have our highly personal motivations for helping others find their own true loves."

"I'm not following you."

GeorgeAnne pushed her glasses farther along the ridge of her nose. "IdaLee was driven to help others find what she never had. Until she reunited with her Charles. ErmaJean became involved because she wanted everyone to know the same happiness she shared for so many years with her beloved late husband."

The old woman fell silent.

"What was your reason, Miss GeorgeAnne?"

She looked at him for a long, long moment. "I help others find their true love because of the love I never knew."

An old wound surfaced in her eyes. "Happened long before your time. The Allens had owned the hardware store for a hundred and fifty years, but my husband wanted no part of it." She gave Colton a level gaze. "He did his best to run it into the ground. Before he ran off with some flatlander passing through town."

Colton stared at her. He'd had no idea. He'd assumed she was a widow like ErmaJean.

"Best thing he ever did for me was give me those boys of mine. Second best thing he ever did was sign over the deed to the store and leave us." She jutted her chin. "I raised them by myself and did a right fine job of it, if I do say so myself."

"Yes, ma'am. You did."

Her "boys" were now middle-aged, respected community leaders with families of their own. The Allens were generous, hardworking, good men.

"It wasn't easy for them growing up without a father." She wagged her finger. "But there's a lot of things worse than nothing. I've never met a strong person who had an easy past."

Colton grimaced.

"Your past doesn't have to define your future. Let it make you better. Learn to see it as a stepping stone to who you were always meant to become." She opened her palms. "Then let go of the pain of it."

"I'm trying, Miss GeorgeAnne." He pinched the bridge of his nose. "I'm trying."

Over the next few days, thanks to the grapevine, the crash and burn of his marriage spread like wildfire. He was glad the truth was out. It saved him having to stumble through awkward explanations of why he and Olly were leaving town. He'd expected to be treated like a pariah by the citizens, but once again the town surprised him. People went out of their way to let him know how much he'd be missed.

Friends checked in with him. Ethan. Luke. Sam. He shared his fears with them about not being the dad Oliver needed. Over the rich aroma of coffee at the Jar, they offered encouragement and prayed with him.

How had it happened that just as he was leaving Truelove, he discovered he had so many more friends than he ever imagined? He dreaded the upcoming appointment with the attorney on Friday. It loomed over him like a coming nightmare.

As for saying goodbye to Mollie forever on Sunday—every time he thought about it he felt like someone had cut off his oxygen.

Colton also decided against taking the beach job. Sand, seagulls and waves no longer held any appeal for him. Despite Mollie's efforts to get rid of him, he and Oliver would only relocate as far as Asheville or Boone.

At heart, he was a mountain guy. And he wanted the same for his son. He might not be able to give Olly Truelove but he could at least give him a Blue Ridge childhood.

Every night, he lay awake into the wee hours. Flat on his back in GeorgeAnne's guest bedroom, he stared at the darkened ceiling. Reliving so many moments with Mollie. Lying there, he took out the memories, one by one, and contemplated the journey they'd been on together since they were children.

In a few days, their journey would end. It was that gnawing realization, more than any uncertainty about his immediate job prospects, that kept him awake at night.

On Wednesday afternoon, he finished an interview with a large construction firm, headquartered in Boone. He sensed they'd offer him the project manager position. He was also considering working toward qualifying for a general contractor's license in the future.

Driving back to Truelove from the high country, he was in no rush to be anywhere. No one was expecting him. Mollie and Oliver were spending the evening with ErmaJean. A chance for her great-aunt to say goodbye.

Pulling off the road, he parked at the trailhead to a rocky promontory overlooking the little town, the river and the bridge. With the first day of summer around the corner, the light lingered long in the sky.

Getting out of the truck, he climbed the path toward the summit. Maybe he'd watch the sunset. And say his own goodbyes. Not only to Truelove, but to a life with Mollie.

Colton sat on the large boulder. The tangy scent of evergreen teased at his nostrils. From here, he could just make out the patch of green on the square. From that fixed point, it wasn't too hard to approximate the location of Mollie's neighborhood. She had been his shining north star for so long, he felt lost without her.

He'd put on a good front for everyone, but he was aching inside. He had the distinct feeling once he drove away from the small mountain hamlet, he would never see her again.

Gravel crunched. Startled, he swung around.

Jack threw up his hand. "I was behind you when your truck turned off the highway. Thought I'd check on you. See how you were doing." He kicked a pebble with the toe of his boot. "I'm sorry about you and Mollie."

He hadn't been able to talk to anyone about the loss of his marriage. Ethan was Mollie's cousin. His first loyalty should be to her.

But for some reason, Colton felt Jack would understand. He found himself pouring out his confusion from beginning to end. Sharing with Jack what Mollie meant to his life.

Colton scrubbed his forehead. "Why do I feel so blindsided and devastated?"

"The end of a marriage feels like a death."

He looked at the former Navy SEAL. "What

I'm feeling is nothing like what you and Kate went through in losing your daughter."

"It was after losing Liddy that Kate and I lost our way with each other. We found ourselves in the same place as you and Mollie. We divorced, or at least we thought we had, until by the grace of God a clerical error gave us a second chance."

Colton squeezed his eyes shut. "I came from such a screwed-up family. Divorce has never been part of the Drakes' vocabulary. It kills me to think about what I've done to Mollie. To all of them."

"God hates divorce, but He has only love and compassion for those who find themselves in that hard place." The cowboy looked at him. "You're an intelligent man. You must've realized how unworkable a marriage of convenience would turn out to be. So why did you ask her to marry you?"

"I was about to be deployed. If I died overseas, I didn't want Oliver to end up in the foster care system."

Jack pursed his lips. "I'm not buying it. What was the real reason? Be honest with yourself."

Colton blinked. "Because… Her mom was diagnosed with cancer. Mollie had decided to move home."

"And?" Jack prompted.

He swallowed. "Because… She'd just broken up with this guy, who I hated by the way."

Jack laughed. "Did you ever like anyone Mollie dated?"

"No," Colton grunted. "But that guy seemed

more significant than the others. She was in a place where she wanted more in her life. I figured once she got to Truelove it wouldn't be long before—" He turned his head.

"Before what?"

"Before I lost her forever." Colton frowned. "When she told me she was returning to Truelove, none of that ran through my head. On some deep instinctual level, I just reacted and asked her to marry me."

Jack nodded. "Gotcha."

"At best, I'm a basket case, aren't I? At worst, a selfish jerk."

Jack quirked his eyebrow. "Why was it so important not to lose your relationship with her?"

Colton frowned. "I told you about what she means to me. Since we were kids."

Jack took off his hat, crimped the brim and settled it on his head again. "Marriage is an extreme reaction to maintaining friendship. You're going to have to do better than that, man. Dig deeper."

Colton turned toward the horizon. "I—I don't know."

"I think you do know. You just won't allow yourself to admit it, much less feel it." Jack leaned against the rock. "Kind of ironic after everything you did to keep your relationship intact, you're losing her now because you're afraid to be honest with yourself."

"I'm sick with fear I've already lost her. I can't sleep. I can't eat."

Jack's gaze bored into his. "Why is that?"

"Because I love her." His chest heaved. "I think I've always loved her."

He nearly gasped at the incredible relief—the freedom—in saying those words aloud.

"It's not me you need to be telling." Jack put his hand on Colton's sleeve. "Tell her how you feel."

Colton's shoulders slumped. "It's too late."

"Take it from a guy who almost left it too late, you've got to tell her. You owe her the truth."

"What if she laughs in my face? What if she says it's too little too late? What if—"

"Are you kidding me?" Jack rolled his eyes. "When the two of you are in a room together, it's obvious to everyone how you feel about each other."

"How do you mean?"

"Dude, it's clear she thinks you hung the moon."

Colton gulped. "You think so? Really?"

"You're just as bad, man." Jack chuckled. "You can't keep from touching her—her hand, her arm, the small of her back."

Her pinkie…

Colton sucked in a breath. Of course. How had he not seen it? Yeah, he'd loved her for a long, long time.

Was Jack right? Was she waiting—had she been waiting—all this time for him to open the door to something more?

Jack crossed his arms. "Bare your heart to her. Beg her forgiveness. See how she responds."

"After everything that's happened, suppose she no longer feels the same?"

"Then at least, you'll know. Once and for all, you'll know where you stand."

"You're right. I have to tell her." He flicked his eyes at the cowboy. "Pray for me."

"For sure." Jack smiled. "If you'd allow me to give you a few words of advice?"

"I could use all the advice I can get."

"Nothing too terribly profound. I'm a cowboy, not a preacher, but here goes." Jack settled against the boulder. "Life is uncertain, and every day is precious."

Colton could hardly bear the sharpness of the pain in his friend's eyes. It was a truth Jack knew the reality of better than most. The mere notion of burying his son the way Jack had buried his beloved daughter sliced like an arrow through Colton's heart.

Removing his Stetson, Jack fingered the brim. "Because every day is precious, spend each one wisely."

A wisdom hard-won.

Jack clamped his hat on his head. "And because we're not promised tomorrow, every day allow yourself to be happy." Smiling at Colton, he adjusted the angle of the brim.

Standing, they got off the rock.

Colton swallowed around the boulder in his throat. "Thank you. For everything." He shook Jack's hand.

He was grateful, so grateful. That God had put new friends into his life. For guys who understood where he was coming from and encouraged him to be real, authentic and honest.

Jack made his departure. Colton decided to catch the sunset somewhere else. Minutes later, he drove toward the church.

The white steeple pierced the dusky sky.

In the empty parking lot, he bared his heart to God. Resting his forehead on the steering wheel, he pleaded for forgiveness and the courage to open himself to being vulnerable with Mollie. With God's help, he confronted the walls he'd erected over the years to shield himself from hurt and pain. And one by one, broke through them until only peace and joy remained.

When he lifted his head, the sky blazed in a breathtaking tapestry of apricot, gold and pink. A dazzling display from the Creator. Whose hand had always and forever guided his life.

His breath caught. "No matter what happens with Mollie, thank You for loving me."

The fiery sunset muted into glorious ribbons of purple and dark indigo. The splendor around him made him long to share it with Mollie.

Why had he kept her at arm's length for so long? What had he been so afraid of? Trusting Mollie with his heart felt like the ultimate risk. But he was ready, for better or worse, to offer her his love. In truth, his heart had been hers almost forever.

He wanted to make a life for Olly in Truelove.

But most of all, he wanted the life he and Mollie could make together. This was his chance to do things the right way. He needed to talk to Ted and Glenda. He also had an appointment with an attorney to cancel.

As the light faded behind the mountain, he was seized with a sudden idea. He must make an effort to show Mollie how much he loved her. Time was running out for them.

He cranked the engine.

But first things first. He headed to town for what promised to be a long-overdue and thoroughly difficult conversation with her parents.

Darkness had fallen. Outside the Drake house, Colton rang the doorbell.

He figured he'd lost back door privileges. The occasion warranted a more formal, front door approach.

Colton smoothed his hand over his head, grateful to be wearing his nicest clothes from the interview that morning.

Ted threw open the door. His eyes widened.

"Before you boot me off your property, Mr. Ted, could I speak to you and Miss Glenda for a few moments?"

Ted rubbed his chin. "We were hoping you'd come say goodbye."

"I didn't come to say goodbye, sir." He swallowed. "I came to ask for your blessing to ask Mollie to marry me."

Ted propped his hands on his hips. "Last I heard, you two are already married."

Mollie's mother peered around her husband. "Let's hear him out, Ted."

Stepping aside, Ted let him pass into the house but they ventured no farther than the foyer. "Okay. We're listening. Give it your best shot."

Not exactly the most encouraging of openings, but…

"Let me start off by apologizing again for not doing right by Mollie all those months ago." He maintained direct eye contact with her father. "I want you to know I love your daughter. I think I always have, but I was afraid loving her would mean losing her."

Glenda touched his arm. "You're not afraid to love her now?"

"No, ma'am." Tears burned at his eyelids. "She is the most wonderful person I've ever known. I can hardly believe she's put up with me all these years. Loved me, too, as impossible as that sounds."

Glenda bit her lip. "She's been equally afraid loving you would mean losing you."

Colton nodded. "She'll never lose me, if she'll give me a second chance. My heart is hers."

Ted's mouth flattened. "Maybe so, but only after breaking her heart in the process."

Glenda took hold of her husband's arm. "Ted…"

"You're right, sir. I don't deserve your forgiveness, but I'm asking for it anyway." He ducked his head. "You took a chance once on a stupid, cocky kid. I'm humbly asking for another to prove how much I love Mollie."

Ted's eyes narrowed. "Talk is cheap, Atkinson."

"Yes, sir. It is. I'll spend the rest of my life making sure she never again regrets loving me. Nor you, either, for opening your family to me."

His heart pounded. The next few minutes would determine the future trajectory of his life. And Olly's. But he was determined to do things the right way this time and if Mollie's parents turned him away, he trusted—hard as it would be—that God had a different, better plan for him, Oliver and Mollie.

Squaring his shoulders, he locked eyes with her father. "But without your blessing, I won't take this any further with Mollie. I'll leave town and never bother her again, if that is what you think is best for her."

For a long, uncomfortable moment, Ted examined him. As was her father's right. If God ever blessed him with a daughter, he would have done the same.

Never breaking eye contact, Colton stood there and let Mollie's dad sift him like wheat from chaff for the truth behind his words. Flaying him open. Holding his feet to the proverbial fire. Drilling down deep to the core of his character.

Please, Lord...

Ted turned to his wife. "How about you do the honors, hon?"

A smile so like Mollie's broke out across Glenda's face. She threw her arms around him. "Welcome to the family, darlin'."

Hugged within an inch of his life, he was so profoundly relieved he sagged in her embrace.

Ted clamped a strong hand on his shoulder. "We were angry and hurt, but we never stopped loving you, son."

"Son" meant more to Colton than words could ever convey.

Ted pulled him into a bear hug. It would take time to mend the damage to his relationship with these dear people, but Colton prayed with God's help they would get there.

"We just had to be sure." Glenda stood back, wiping tears from her eyes. "Tell us how you plan to make this right with Mollie. And if there's anything we can do to help."

He explained his idea. Mollie's parents were quick to lend their support. As he was about to leave to head over to GeorgeAnne's, Ted pulled him aside.

"You proved yourself an asset to Drake Construction." Mollie's father touched his shoulder. "You may have found other work you prefer, but I hope you'll consider coming on board in a permanent capacity as my right-hand man. Make it a true second-generation family business." Ted held up his hands. "No pressure, though, if that's not something you want. But I do hope you'll think about my offer."

"I don't have to think about it, sir." His heart

warmed by her father's continuing generosity, Colton shook his hand. "Thank you. There's nothing I'd love more than working and learning alongside you every day."

"We can talk through the details later." Ted smiled. "I look forward to the two of us taking Drake Construction to the next level."

Colton, too.

He returned to his truck. For Mollie's sake, he needed help—a lot of help—to pull this off. Time to gather reinforcements.

It was time—he could hardly believe he was thinking this—to call in the matchmakers.

Chapter Fourteen

Colton found GeorgeAnne in her kitchen.

"Well?" she barked. "I can tell from your face something's happened. Spit it out."

He took a deep breath. "I love her, Miss GeorgeAnne."

The older woman sniffed. "A surprise to no one but yourself." She skewered him with a glance. "What I really want to know is what you aim to do about it?"

For the second time that evening, he sketched out his idea. "What do you think?"

She smirked. "I think imitation is the sincerest form of flattery."

"What?"

"By reminding her of happy times in the past, it may soften her up to accepting your proposal. By the way, you're welcome."

He cocked his head. "For what?"

"The milestone strategy." She fluttered her hand. "You two didn't actually believe you were fooling anyone, did you?"

"Excuse me?"

"Did you think we were born yesterday?" She cackled. "We saw through your so-called marriage of convenience soon after Mollie and Oliver arrived in Truelove. Before you ever returned. That girl of yours never could tell a convincing lie. She wears her heart on her sleeve."

His eyes widened. "You knew?"

"On fun-due night, the guest bedroom confirmed our suspicions." She wagged her finger. "Never try to kid a kidder, Atkinson."

"Ted and Glenda—"

"Bless their dear trusting hearts, Mollie's parents were probably the only ones who didn't realize the truth. Only because of everything else they were dealing with."

He shook his head. "But when I took over planning the date nights—"

"Just as we hoped you would." She grinned. "The couples massage was IdaLee's stroke of genius. Tipped you right over the edge into taking the lead."

Colton blinked. "That day at the Jar with Martha Alice and CoraFaye, you staged the whole thing?"

"You walked right into that one," she crowed. "Face it, Atkinson. You've been outplayed and outwitted by a bunch of old women."

He gaped at her. "I cannot believe you…"

"Engagements of convenience. Marriages of convenience. Been there, done both." She lifted her bony chin. "The matchmakers were committed to getting you two to acknowledge how much you loved each other. And it worked. Although, I'm not too proud to admit you've been our toughest match thus far."

"There's no happily-ever-after yet." He sighed. "I need your help, Miss GeorgeAnne."

"You need more than my help. We're going to have to run this up the flagpole of the Double Name Club. If they're game, we're a go."

He touched her sleeve. "Thank you for your efforts to bring Mollie and I together."

Never one to tolerate sentimentality of any sort, she reached for her phone on the countertop. "You had only to come home to find each other."

The next morning, GeorgeAnne called an emergency Double Name Club meeting at the Jar. When he arrived, the women were already waiting for him at their table by the bulletin board. Taking a seat, he explained his vision for making his proposal to Mollie a day she would never forget.

"Is this a terrible idea?" He opened his hands. "Will this even work?"

CoraFaye Dolan sniffed. "It is extremely last minute."

Martha Alice Breckenridge pursed her lips. "Pulling it off may be difficult."

IdaLee put a hand to her snow-white hair. "And requires an enormous amount of coordination." Her lips twitched.

"Wait." His gaze cut to GeorgeAnne. "Y'all are playing me again, aren't you?"

The ladies burst into mischievous laughter.

"One born every minute," CoraFaye hooted.

"If you could have seen your face." Glorieta slapped her thigh.

Martha Alice threw her friends a slightly wicked grin. "It never gets old, does it?"

Yet he couldn't find it in himself to be angry. He reckoned he'd had it coming.

"Take heart, honey." ErmaJean patted his hand. "Nothing worth having is ever easily won."

"It's never wise to underestimate the Double Name Club." GeorgeAnne pushed her glasses higher on her nose. "You do realize the significance of Friday's date?"

His eyes found hers. "Our first-year anniversary. If you recall, I did promise to bring you in on the planning. Will you help me?"

"Don't I always?" Something approaching fondness—probably just his imagination—softened her steely gaze. "Of course, I'll help you. Let's do this."

Over the next hour, they outlined a workable plan. The grapevine proved incredibly useful. Phone calls were made. Troops were rallied. Mollie's friends dropped by to lend a hand.

Naturally, GeorgeAnne took charge of organizing the volunteers. AnnaBeth was tasked with decorations.

"Mollie likes pink," he reminded the statuesque style maven.

"There'll be oodles of pink," AnnaBeth promised.

He wrote down the specific information to be

included, but he left the creation of the signs to Truelove's resident artist, Lila. She would have one of the most important roles in pulling off the surprise for Mollie.

"You'll let everyone know when to arrive?" He looked at Maggie Hollingsworth. "She loves people."

Wilda Arledge, Maggie's mother-in-law, squeezed his hand. "Don't you worry. We've got it covered."

Myra Penry jotted a note on a pad of paper. "The more, the merrier."

Shayla would serenade them. Callie McAbee signed on to take photos. Kara MacKenzie offered to cater the engagement party.

He sighed. "Are we sure there will be an engagement party? That she won't just throw me out on my ear?"

Amber, who would be on Olly-duty before placing him in the care of the Dolans, rolled her eyes. "Not going to happen."

He frowned. "I just want everything to be perfect for her."

"It can't help but be perfect." Kate Dolan smiled. "Because it will be coming from you."

He wished he shared their confidence. If Mollie turned him away, he wasn't sure how he would go on from there.

Early on Friday, everyone gathered for final instructions at ErmaJean's house. GeorgeAnne handed out the timeline and gave everyone their assigned locations.

He was beyond touched that their friends had taken off work and even made alternate arrangements for childcare to help him make this happen.

A lump settled in his throat. "Mollie is going to feel so loved. Thank you."

Sam fist-bumped his shoulder. "Hey, man, it's not just Mollie we love."

Colton was so grateful for everything God had done for him and in him through the good people of Truelove.

Then it was time. Lila headed out to initiate the first phase of Operation Proposal—getting Mollie away from the house so the decorating could begin.

That week, Mollie spent as much time with Olly as possible. Tears were never far from the surface. She hid them the best she could, but she worried Oliver sensed something wasn't right.

The days rushed by. Too soon, it would be Father's Day. She would have to say goodbye to the child she couldn't have loved more if he was her own.

Over the course of small, teachable moments, she tried to prepare the little boy for their ultimate separation. For a life without her.

She talked to him about how he was going on a wonderful trip with his dad soon.

"Won't it be fun to feel the sand between your piggies?" With a deliberate effort of will, she injected enthusiasm into her voice. "You and Daddy can build sandcastles together."

Olly shrugged. “Ride horsie.”

She looked at him. Where had that come from? “Not horses, sweetie. You and Daddy will ride in his truck to the beach.”

Zooming his miniature cars around on the rug, Oliver shook his head. “No, Mommy. Ride horsie.”

Apparently, the pony ride at the picnic made a big impression. If horses were the only thing he remembered from that awful day, though, she was glad.

She canceled her Friday appointments so she could spend more time with him. She was washing the breakfast dishes when Lila showed up at the back door.

“I’m so glad I caught you at home. Hey, Olly.” Lila waved. “And Blue.”

Olly played on the floor with his plastic dinosaurs and his dog.

“Get a gander at you.” Smiling, Mollie turned off the faucet. “All gussied up in heels and a dress. What’s the occasion?”

Lila pinked becomingly. “Sam and I are going to a party later, and I was wondering if you’d do me a favor.”

She nodded. “Sure. If I can. What’s up?”

“When I told your mom how I haven’t seen my toes for quite some time, she offered to give me a pedicure this morning.” Lila beamed at her. “I’ll be her first mani-pedi client at Hair Raisers.”

“That sounds great.” Mollie tilted her head. “How can I help?”

"It would be more fun if you came, too." Lila wound a curly lock of her bright red hair around her finger. "A Girls' Day Out before the baby comes."

"Under other circumstances I'd love to, but I've cleared my schedule to spend the day with Oliver."

There was a sharp rap on the door.

"Come in," she called. Blue woofed a greeting.

"Hey, y'all." Amber strolled into the kitchen. "I was wondering if Olly could play with Parker today."

Oliver abandoned the dinosaurs. "Parker?"

Amber gave him a big smile. "Would you like to play with Parker today?"

"Wait a minute." She frowned. "Olly and I are spending the day together."

Lila threw her a smile. "If Oliver is heading out with Amber, you're free to do a Girls' Day with me, right?"

"Sorry. No can do." She folded her arms. "Olly and I already have plans."

Oliver tugged at the hem of her T-shirt. "Parker."

Her forehead creased. "Sweetie pie, don't you want to stay home with Mommy this morning?"

The little boy shook his head. "Parker."

Her heart pinched. Was she being selfish? Other people loved Olly, too. This would probably be his last chance to play with his little cousin. She should be happy he wasn't clinging to her. Instead, she felt like bursting into tears.

She bit her lip. "I—I guess it would be okay if Oliver spent the day with Parker..."

Amber patted her arm. "He'll have lots of fun. You and Lila have fun, too."

"But Father's Day is coming so fast…"

"You need a distraction." Lila clasped her hands together. "Getting a mani-pedi will make you feel better. Please?"

Mollie doubted anything would make her feel better, but she didn't want to be a killjoy.

She swallowed. "It could be fun…"

Amber and Olly turned to go.

"Wait." She leaped forward. "What about his bag?"

Amber smiled. "I've got everything he'll need for today."

"Olly?" She put her hand on his cheek. "Don't I get a hug?"

Amber nudged him. "Tell Mommy goodbye."

He threw his arms around her legs and just as quickly let go. "Bye, Mommy. Ride horsie."

Amber and Lila exchanged a look.

What was with Olly and the horses?

She flushed. "Apparently, he's moved from bears to a new obsession."

At the door, Amber paused with Oliver. "See you about four."

Mollie waggled her fingers. "Bye, sweetie—"

The screen door banged shut behind them. *Okay.* Feeling slightly discarded, she had a hard time keeping the ever-present tears at bay.

"Girls' Day Out demands more than shorts and a T-shirt." Grabbing her arm, Lila tugged her toward

Mollie's bedroom. "Let's see what we can find in your closet. You should wear something that makes you feel happy."

After Sunday came and went, she had serious doubts she'd ever feel happy again.

Lila pulled out a summery white dress. "What about this one?"

Her pulse skittered.

A midi dress, the tiered dress of softest cotton had a flirty hem and ruffled sleeves. She'd only worn it once. The day she and Colton got married at the courthouse.

Despite the circumstances, she recalled the day with great happiness. The dress had made her feel feminine. She also remembered how Colton's eyes lit up when he saw her in it.

She wouldn't mind feeling like that again—happy and full of hope. She reached for it. "Why not?"

The next few hours were a whirlwind. Lila insisted on driving. At Hair Raisers, her mother's face wore a special glow. "Thank you both for letting me practice my skills."

Lila laughed. "My pleasure. Is a foot massage included?"

Mollie's mom chuckled. "Absolutely."

The mani-pedis were fun. Trying out different colors before settling on their favorites, she and Lila laughed a lot. Around lunchtime, Glorieta dropped off a platter of chicken salad sandwiches, cut into triangles.

"Kara's catering an engagement party tonight." Glorieta winked at her mom. "That girl of mine always makes a-plenty. I wanted to share. Y'all enjoy. Better get back and help her." The older African American lady bustled out.

After lunch, Lila wanted them to do each other's makeup. Mollie was agreeable, but she kept a watchful eye on the time. When the makeup session was over, her mother insisted on doing their hair. Lila went first, then Mollie took her turn in the chair.

Standing behind her, Mollie's mom smiled at their reflections. "How's it feel being on this side of the chair?"

"A little odd," she admitted.

But if the mani-pedi-spa thing could make her mother look this happy and excited, she was delighted to oblige.

Her mom ran practiced fingers through the length of Mollie's hair. "I think I'll take the weight off the ends and shape it up, if that's all right with you."

She settled into the chair. "I'll be happy with whatever you do."

Forty minutes later, she stared at herself in the mirror. "Wow, Mom." She twisted her neck to get a better view. "Pretty glamorous for a Friday afternoon in Truelove."

Her mother smiled. "Do you like it?"

"I love it."

Her mom whisked the pink cape off Mollie. "I love you." She spun the chair around so they faced each other.

Was there a sheen of tears in her mom's eyes?

"I love you, too, Mom."

Her mother gave her the tenderest of smiles. "Be happy, my sweet girl."

"Is everything all right?"

She kissed Mollie's cheek. "Everything's perfect."

Glancing at the clock, Mollie vaulted from the chair. "It's almost four o'clock. Oliver's due back. I need to get home."

"Of course." Lila grabbed her purse. "Thank you so much, Miss Glenda, for this wonderful day." Yet she appeared in no hurry to depart.

Lila and her mother exchanged—in her opinion—overly protracted farewells. Mollie fought her growing exasperation. She had to drag the expectant redhead out to Lila's car.

"I really need to get home," Mollie pleaded. "ASAP."

But moving at a snail's pace, her friend made much ado about getting into the vehicle, then slowly pulling the seat belt across her protruding belly. Eventually, Lila pulled away from the salon. Yet instead of heading down Main, she took a right at the corner of the square.

"Where are you going?" Mollie gripped the armrest. "This isn't the way home."

"In the glove box, there's a note from Colton. He wanted you to read it now."

"What?" Mollie gaped at her. "Is this some kind of joke? Where's Oliver?"

"It's no joke. I promise you'll see Olly in the next few minutes." Lila nudged her chin at the console. "But go ahead. Read it."

"Colton left me a note—you're only now telling me—" She tore open the glove box.

A white envelope with her name written in Colton's all-business, block-style print lay on top of the owner's manual. Sliding her finger under the flap, she removed the single piece of white stationery paper.

Molls, I love you.

Inhaling sharply, she put her hand to her mouth.

> Please forgive the hurt I've caused you. For me, truly the longest road out has been the shortest road home. A road that always leads me to you. I hope you enjoy reliving the journey as much as I've loved spending it with you. See you soon. I'll be waiting for you with much love in my heart. Yours forever, Colton.

Tears stinging her eyes, she looked at Lila. "What's happening?"

Slowing the car to a crawl, Lila smiled. "One of the best days of your life, sweet friend."

Engine running, Lila stopped the car outside the school playground. On the sidewalk, a beaming IdaLee and her Charles stood arm in arm. The retired schoolteacher held a sign. *Our story begins here, Molls...*

The poster also contained a date—the long ago

day she met Colton on the playground. Tears trickled down her cheeks.

Lila handed her a tissue and put the car in motion once more. They continued around the square. Clients and friends held lots of posters. Each one marked a milestone of her journey with Colton.

Outside the Mason Jar, Trudy's poster said *Milkshakes.* Making a full circuit of the green, Lila drove past additional signs. *The Burger Barn. Karaoke. Fish Tacos.*

Was this really happening?

Blurry-eyed, she gazed out the window. Smiling through her tears. Waving. Mouthing "thank you." Soaking in the love and support.

Lila turned into their neighborhood. Outside the Gibson house, Emma Cate blew her a kiss. Sam grinned. His sign read *The Pond.*

Across the street, Mrs. Desmond and her Chihuahua stood with AnnaBeth and Jonas Stone. The poster he carried read *The Waterfall.* She dabbed at her eyes.

Farther down the block, she spotted Luke and little Jeremiah. *Picnics.* Beyond the Morgans, her cousin Ethan and the twins. *Hiking.*

So many wonderful memories of her journey from friendship to something more with Colton. Mollie laughed at GeorgeAnne's poster. *Fun-due Night.*

Near the bottom of her driveway, Oliver sat tall and proud on the back of a pony. On either side, Jack and Kate Dolan stood with him.

So he had been right about riding a horse today.

Colton must have coached him. The little boy had somehow managed not to spill the beans.

Olly's face broke into a grin. Taking one hand off the saddle horn, he waved. She winced. But keeping a firm hand on his back, Kate winked to let her know all was well.

Lila steered into the driveway and shut off the engine. Standing in front of her house, Aunt EJ held one last poster. *Today is the day our love story truly begins...*

She fanned her face. Did this mean what she thought it meant?

Her father opened the car door. "Mollie girl." He offered his hand. "There is a young man waiting rather desperately to ask you a question."

She stepped out of the car. "Oh, Daddy."

Her father tucked her hand into the crook of his arm. They walked around the house toward the backyard. Her knees wobbled.

Stopping at the back gate, her father removed her hand. "This is as far as your old man goes." When he smiled, tears of happiness leaked out of his eyes.

"I trust Colton to take it from here. But you'll always..." His voice caught. "You'll always be my Mollie girl. I love you, sweetheart. Be happy." He kissed her cheek and left her there.

Praying Lila's makeup job had withstood the tears, she swiped her eyes. She tucked a tendril of hair behind her ear.

Then she went through the garden gate to the man she'd loved forever.

* * *

From her vantage point on the deck, Shayla must have seen Mollie arrive. She began playing a song on her guitar. Colton's cue. Callie McAbee and her camera hovered on the periphery, ready to document the moment.

So far, so good. Everything had gone like clockwork. Later, he knew Mollie would enjoy hearing the behind-the-scenes details of how it all came together.

Just then, Mollie and her father rounded the corner of the house.

Lila had followed Colton's instructions to the letter. He'd asked her to direct Mollie into selecting a particular dress. The same dress she'd worn when they legally became husband and wife.

But this time—this time he was ready to really mean it. To honor and love her and give her all of himself.

Alone, Mollie stepped forward into the dappled light of the mid-June afternoon. His heart hitched. The air left his lungs in a rush.

Everything else fell away. The soft, romantic music. The whir of the camera's shutter. There existed for Colton only her and him.

At the end of a grassy aisle lined with flickering white candles, he stood there, wearing a tie and his best suit. His hands laced in front of him. Terrified. Excited.

Her gaze locked onto his. His heart thundered.

She smiled at him. And that was when he knew everything was going to be all right.

She walked down the aisle of candles to him. He took hold of her hands. His eyelids pricked with emotion.

"Molls," he rasped. "You are the most beautiful person, inside and out, I've ever met."

Her eyes shone.

"You are my first thought in the morning and my last at night. You're an amazing, funny, smart, wonderful woman." His voice thickened. "I am so thankful God put you in my life. I love you, Mollie Drake."

She choked back a sob. "I love you, too, Colton."

"You're the most generous, welcoming person I've ever known. You never fail to be there for friends going through hard times. I've long counted it a privilege to be the first of those friends."

"And the best," she murmured.

"Just by being you, you make everyone around you happy. You make me so happy, Molls." He closed his eyes for a moment. "It's taken me far too long to get to this place with you. There's been far too many detours."

"Not too many. Just enough. No more than necessary." She squeezed his hands. "God's timing is always perfect."

He smiled at her. "Looking back, I think I had to go away, out into the world, to appreciate how wonderful home could be."

Lifting her hand, he brushed his lips against her fingers. "You are my home, Mollie."

The love in her eyes for him, none of which he deserved, nearly felled him.

"I wanted to make sure this time you received the proposal you deserved. With our family and friends here to witness me tell you how much I love you."

He let go of her hands.

Reaching in his pocket, he withdrew a small black box and went down on one knee. She touched her hand to her chest.

"I would be the most blessed man on earth to be able to call you my wife and to have you by my side for the rest of my life." He opened the box. "Mollie Frances Drake, would you marry me? This time for all the right reasons. A real marriage in the eyes of God." His heart in his throat, he looked at her.

With the sweetest of smiles, she leaned forward and caught his face in her hands. "Yes, Colton Edward Atkinson. A thousand times, yes."

She kissed him.

He slipped the engagement ring on her finger. A diamond ring he'd bought yesterday with guidance from Mollie's mom.

Jumping to his feet, he grabbed hold of Mollie and swung her around. They were both laughing and crying. He'd never known he could be this happy.

"She said yes!" he hollered and fist-pumped the air.

The post-proposal engagement party erupted.

Everyone they knew in Truelove, and then some, poured out of the house into the backyard. There was a melee of children. Several ecstatic, barking canines. Reams of food, under Kara's supervision, were deposited onto the linen-draped tables under the canopy of trees around the perimeter of the yard.

Her parents were the first to congratulate them.

Dashing forward, Oliver lifted his arms to him. "Daddy!"

His heart full, he held his boy close.

A steady stream of well-wishers followed. Including the Double Name Club, eager to claim bragging rights. Mollie was totally in her element. As for him…

Thanks to her influence, he was learning not to mind people so much.

In her Sunday best—Colton wasn't sure he'd ever actually seen GeorgeAnne in a dress before—the matchmaker strolled by with a plate of smoked salmon sandwiches, cut into fancy triangles.

He caught her arm. "Thank you, Miss GeorgeAnne. For everything."

She laid her gnarled, work-calloused hand against his cheek. "Love each other well, my dearest boy. That will be thanks enough."

His eyes moistened.

But her gaze had fixed on a disturbance happening over his shoulder. "Austin and Logan Hollingsworth!" She harangued her much-loved six-year-old great-nephews. "You will cease and desist this instant."

And she was off to toughly love another generation of Truelove troublemakers.

Mollie threw him a happy smile.

He couldn't wait to see what else God had for him, Mollie and their family.

Their story—their journey—had come full circle. And the most beautiful thing about a circle?

It had no end.

Oliver Edward Atkinson and Blue
Request the Honor of Your Company
At the Wedding of

Mollie Frances Drake
&
Colton Edward Atkinson

August 1
Truelove, North Carolina

* * * * *

Dear Reader,

I hope you had as much fun reading about Colton and Mollie's fun-due night as I had in writing that scene. For me, their story boiled down to three truths:

1. Each day is precious.
2. Therefore, spend each one wisely.
3. Allow yourself to be happy.

Because God is my faithful Creator, I can entrust Him with every circumstance. He will always do what is best and right for me. I need not fear the future. I'm also training my eyes to delight in the glimmers of joy He places in my path each day—like a bright red cardinal on an evergreen branch, a delicately winged monarch butterfly or the majestic purple petals of a flower opening to the sun.

Thank you for sharing Colton, Mollie and Oliver's journey with me. It is through Christ we find our forever Home—the true Happily-Ever-After for which we were created. Thank you for telling your friends how much you enjoy the Truelove matchmaker series.

I'd love to connect with you. You can contact me at lisa@lisacarterauthor.com or visit lisacarterauthor.com, where you can also subscribe to my author newsletter for news about upcoming book releases and sales.

In His Love,
Lisa